THE ROVER BOYS DOWN EAST

OR

THE STRUGGLE FOR THE STANHOPE FORTUNE

BY
ARTHUR M. WINFIELD

NEW WEST PRESS

Copyright © 2022 by New West Press

ISBN 978-1-64965-116-7

All rights reserved. This book or any portion thereof may not be reproduced or used in any manner whatsoever without the express written permission of the publisher except for the use of brief quotations in a book review or scholarly journal.

New West Press
Henderson, NV 89052
www.nwwst com

Ordering Information:
Special discounts are available on quantity purchases by corporations, associations, educators, and others. For details, contact the publisher at the listed address below.

U.S. trade bookstores and wholesalers: Please contact New West Press:

Tel: (480) 648-1061; or email: contact@nwwst.com

INTRODUCTION

My Dear Boys: This is a complete story in itself, but forms the fifteenth volume of the "Rover Boys Series for Young Americans."

Twelve years ago the line was started with the publication of the first three stories, "The Rover Boys at School," "On the Ocean," and "In the Jungle." I earnestly hoped that the young people would like the tales, but never did I anticipate the tremendously enthusiastic welcome which was given to the volumes from the start, nor the steady sale, ever increasing, which has been accorded the series up to the present time. The publication of the first three books immediately called for a fourth, "The Rover Boys Out West," and then followed yearly "On the Great Lakes," "In Camp," "On Land and Sea," "On the River," "On the Plains," "In Southern Waters," "On the Farm," "On Treasure Isle," and then "At College," where we last left our heroes.

Dick, Tom and Sam are older than when we first made their acquaintance and told how they went to Putnam Hall. They are now college boys, attending a well-known institution of learning in the middle-west. But though older, they are as lively as ever, and Tom, at least, is just as full of fun. They have a great struggle to save the Stanhope fortune, and have to work hard to get the best of several enemies. They take a long journey Down East, and their adventures are both mysterious and exciting.

Again I take this opportunity to thank my friends, both young and old, for all the nice things they have said about my books. I am more than sorry that I cannot answer all the letters that pour in upon me from everywhere praising the stories. I earnestly hope the present volume will please all my readers and do them some good.

Affectionately and sincerely yours,

EDWARD STRATEMEYER

CONTENTS

I. A Game Of Baseball	1
II. The Fire On The Steamer	8
III. College Boys To The Rescue	14
IV. What Flockley Had To Tell	21
V. A Celebration On The Campus	27
VI. Good-Bye To Brill	34
VII. Dreams Of Youth	40
VIII. Home Once More	46
IX. Preparations For The Fourth Of July	52
X. When The Cannon Went Off	58
XI. A Day To Remember	65
XII. Off For Camp	71
XIII. Hans Mueller's Queer Catch	77
XIV. The Happenings Of A Night	83
XV. Strange News	89
XVI. Something Of A Clue	95
XVII. Dan Baxter's Revelation	101
XVIII. A Fortune And A Lady Disappear	107
XIX. On The Way To Boston	114
XX. An Adventure In Boston	121
XXI. From One Clue To Another	127
XXII. A Chase Up The Coast	133
XXIII. Aboard The Mary Delaway	138
XXIV. Out On Casco Bay	143
XXV. On Chesoque Island	148
XXVI. A Talk Of Importance	153
XXVII. What Happened In The Cave	158
XXVIII. At The Bottom Of The Pool	163
XXIX. A Minute Too Late	168
XXX. Back Home—Conclusion	173

"WELL, NOW THE TENT IS FIXED, AND WE'LL HAVE SUPPER,"
SAID DICK.

CHAPTER I

A GAME OF BASEBALL

"Hurrah! that's the way to do it!"

"Now, then, Tom, see if you can't bring Dick home!"

"Give him a swift one, Frank! Don't let him hit it!" cried Sam Rover, merrily.

"I'll knock it down into the river!" retorted Tom Rover, as he caught up a bat and walked to the home plate.

"I'm waiting for you, Tom!" sang out Dick Rover, who had just reached second base on a beautiful drive to right field. "Come now, it's time we tied the score."

"Everybody in the game!" yelled Stanley Browne, who was in the coacher's box. "Here is where we do 'em up!"

"Get ready to run, Dick!" came from Songbird Powell. "Tom is going to land it on the other side of the river."

"If he does that I'll walk home," answered Dick, with a grin.

"Now then, here is where Tom misses!" called out Sam, who was behind the bat, and he thumped his fist in his catcher's mitt. "Give him a double-ender curve, Frank."

"Oh, I'll give him a regular corkscrew curl," retorted Frank Holden, who occupied the pitcher's box. "Tom, prepare to die!" And he drew back to pitch the ball.

Eighteen of the students of Brill College were having a game of baseball on the athletic field of that institution of learning. The regular season for baseball was at an end, and the youths had fixed up their nines to suit themselves, with Dick Rover as captain of one side and Frank Holden as captain on the other. On Dick's side were his brother Tom, and a number of their chums, while Sam was doing the catching for Frank.

It was only a friendly contest and all of the students were in the best of spirits. The main examinations for the term were practically over, and in a few days more the students were to scatter for the summer vacation.

It was the ending of the fourth inning and the score stood 6 to 4 in favor of Frank Holden's nine. If Tom should manage to bring both Dick and himself in it would tie the score. But Tom was not known for his home-run qualities.

Frank Holden made a signal to Sam and then sent in a low, swift ball. Tom made a swing at it. But he was too slow.

"Strike one!" sang out Will Faley, the umpire. "Try it some more, Tom."

Again the ball came in and this time Tom struck at it with all his might.

Crack! The ashen stick met the horsehide and the ball went whizzing off to the right of the home plate, in the direction of a number of students who were crossing the grounds.

"Foul!" sang out the umpire, as the sphere curved through the air.

"You can't get it, Sam!" called out Max Spangler. "It's too far off already!"

"Look out, you fellows!" yelled Frank, from the pitcher's box. "If you don't——"

Before he could finish the crowd walking across the grounds looked up and commenced to scatter, to give Sam a chance to catch the ball, which had gone quite high in the air. But before the youngest Rover could reach the sphere down it came—straight on the fancy straw hat of a dudish youth, crushing the article over its wearer's head.

"Whoop! there's a strike for you, Tom!" murmured Dick.

"Do you call that knocking the ball over the river?" demanded Songbird, dryly.

"Here's a case where a straw shows how the ball blows," misquoted Stanley Browne.

"Hi! hi! what do you mean by smashing my hat!" roared Dudd

Flockley, the student who had been thus assaulted. "Who did this, I demand to know?"

"I knocked the ball—but I didn't aim for your hat," answered Tom. And as Dudd Flockley held up the damaged hat he could not help but grin.

"You did it on purpose, Tom Rover!" growled the dudish student. "You needn't deny it!"

"Nonsense, Dudd!" put in Stanley. "He wanted to make a home run—he wasn't aiming at your hat at all."

"I know better!" answered the other student, bitterly. "Say, Tom Rover, it's up to you to buy me a new hat," he added.

"All right, if that's the way you feel about it," answered Tom. "You get the hat and I'll pay for it. But I didn't smash it on purpose, Dudd."

"That hat cost me five dollars, and I don't know where to get one like it," growled the dudish pupil.

"Oh, I can tell you where to get a hat like that!" piped in a drawling voice. "Try the Melrose English Shop, on Broadway. They have all styles, don't you know."

"Good for William Philander Tubbs!" cried Dick. "He knows the directory on straw hats."

"Huh! Think I'm going all the way to New York for a new hat?" growled Dudd Flockley. "I want one to go home in."

"Maybe I can lend you an old one," suggested Tom, dryly.

"I don't want your old hat," growled Dudd Flockley. "I'll get a new one—and you can foot the bill!" and he turned and walked away, his face full of sourness.

"The same old Flockley," whispered Sam to his brother. "After all we did for him, too!"

"You beware of Dudd," put in Songbird, who was near. "He pretends to be friendly, since you put in a good word for him to the doctor, but, just the same, he has got it in for you."

"Play ball!" called out the umpire; and then the ball was thrown down to Frank Holden, and the game went on. Tom gave one more glance in the direction of Dudd Flockley and saw that the dudish student had stopped in his walk, turned around, and was glaring at him savagely.

To my old readers the lads who have thus far taken a part in this story will need no special introduction. But for the benefit of others who have not read the former volumes in this "Rover Boys Series," let me state that Dick, Tom and Sam Rover were three brothers, who, when at home, lived with their father, Anderson Rover, and their Uncle Randolph and Aunt Martha, on a beautiful farm called Valley Brook.

From the farm, and while their father was in Africa, the three boys had been sent to a military academy, as related in the first volume of this series, called "The Rover Boys at School." At the school they made a large number of friends, and also a few enemies, and had "the best time ever," as Sam expressed it.

A term at school was followed by a trip on the ocean, as set down in the second volume of this series, and then by a journey to Africa, where the boys went to locate their father, who had become a captive of the natives. After that came a trip out West, to locate a mine belonging to the Rovers, and then trips to the Great Lakes, and to the mountains, and then, returning to the school, the lads went into camp with the other cadets.

"I guess we had better settle down now," said Dick. But this was not to be. Not much later they took a long trip on land and sea, and followed this up by a voyage on the Ohio and the Mississippi Rivers on a flatboat. Then came some thrilling adventures on the plains, and a little later found the dauntless boys in Southern waters, where they solved the mystery of a deserted steam yacht.

"The farm for mine!" said Tom, after traveling north from the Gulf, and all of the boys were glad to take it easy for some weeks, and also get ready to graduate from Putnam Hall. They had an idea they were to go directly from the military school to college. But something turned up which made them change their plans.

Through Mr. Rover it was learned that a small fortune belonging to a certain Stanhope estate was missing. It had been secreted on an island of the West Indies, and it was settled that the Rovers and some of their friends should go in quest of it.

The boys were particularly anxious to locate this treasure, and with good reason. While at Putnam Hall they had made the acquaintance of Dora Stanhope and also of Nellie and Grace Laning, Dora's cousins. From the very start Dick was attracted to Dora, and now the pair were practically engaged to be married. Tom had taken a particular liking to Nellie Laning and it must be confessed that Sam was equally smitten with Grace.

It was learned that the treasure had been willed to Mr. Stanhope, and consequently, on his death, it had become part of his estate, which in turn had been willed in part to his wife and Dora, with a small share to Mrs. Laning, his sister.

"We'll get that treasure and make the girls happy," declared Dick, and how the whole crowd set off on the quest has already been told in the thirteenth volume of this series, entitled: "The Rover Boys on Treasure Isle." The treasure was also claimed by two of their enemies, Sid Merrick and his nephew, Tad Sobber, and they did all they could to gain possession of the valuables. But the treasure was at last brought safely to this country, and then it was learned that Sid Merrick had been lost at sea in a hurricane. Tad Sobber was saved, and carried on a passing vessel to England.

"And now for college!" cried all of the Rover boys, and wondered to what institution of learning they were to go.

"How would you like to go to Brill?" asked Mr. Rover. "It is a fine place, located in one of our middle-western states, and the head of it, Doctor John Wallington, is an old friend of mine."

The boys had heard that Dora, Grace and Nellie were going to an institution known as Hope Seminary, not far from the town of Ashton. As soon as they learned that Brill College was situated less than two miles from Hope they decided without hesitation to go to the institution their parent had mentioned.

"We'll be near the girls, and we ought to have lots of good times," said Tom.

"It will be our own fault if we don't," Dick had answered.

How the brothers went to Brill has already been related in the volume entitled "The Rover Boys at College." At Brill, as at Putnam Hall, they quickly made a number of friends, not the least of whom were Stanley Browne, Max Spangler, a German student, and Allen Charter, the leading senior. They also had with them their former school chums, John Powell, better known as Songbird because of his cleverness in writing and reciting doggerel, and William Philander Tubbs, a student whose entire spare time was spent in buying things to wear of the latest fashions, and in seeking the society of his young lady friends.

At Brill the Rovers soon came into contact with the dudish pupil, Dudd Flockley, and also with two bullies, Jerry Koswell and Bart Larkspur. Led by Koswell, who was a thoroughly bad egg, the three tried their best to make trouble for the Rovers, and finally succeeded. But the rascals overreached themselves, and when they were exposed Koswell and Larkspur became so frightened that they ran away from Brill and refused to return. Dudd Flockley remained, and he pleaded so earnestly to be forgiven that the Rovers finally decided to drop the case against him, and spoke a good word for him to the head of the college, and he was allowed to continue at Brill.

"I guess Flockley has learned his lesson," said Dick. But it looked as if he might be mistaken, for Flockley, as soon as he felt himself secure at Brill, acted in anything but a grateful manner. Yet he was not as assertive as he had been, for he missed the companionship and support of his former cronies.

With the fortune in their possession, and Sid Merrick dead, the Stanhopes and Lanings had felt secure of their wealth. But, returning from England, Tad Sobber had gone to a shyster lawyer, and put in a claim, and the lawyer had obtained a court injunction, restraining anybody from touching a dollar of the money. This depressed the girls greatly, and made them, for a time, leave Hope. But in the end, the injunction was dissolved, and the Stanhopes and Lanings were told that they could do as they pleased with the fortune.

"That's the best news yet!" Dick had said, on hearing it. "I guess that will put a spoke in Tad Sobber's wheel."

"It will take one out, you mean," returned Tom, with a sly grin. "Wonder what Tad will do next?"

"He can't do anything," had come from Sam. "He is knocked out clean and clear. I always said he had no right to the fortune. That claim of Sid Merrick's was a fake pure and simple."

"I believe you," Dick answered. "Just the same, I feel, somehow, that Tad won't give up even yet."

"But what can he do?" his two brothers had asked.

"I don't know—but he'll try to do something; see if he doesn't."

A few days later had come in some particulars of the case. After the injunction had been dissolved Tad Sobber and his lawyer had gotten into a big row and Sobber had ended by blackening the legal gentleman's left eye. Then Sobber had mysteriously disappeared, but the next day he had sent a rambling letter to Mrs. Stanhope, stating that, even if thrown out of court, he considered that the fortune from Treasure Isle belonged to him, and, sooner or later, he meant to gain possession of it.

"We'll have to watch out for Tad Sobber," had been Dick's comment, on learning the news. "He is growing desperate, and there is no telling what he will do next."

"He's the same old sneak he was at Putnam Hall," declared Tom.

"This will scare Mrs. Stanhope, and Mrs. Laning, too," had been Sam's comment.

"And the girls," his oldest brother had added. "I wish we could round Tad Sobber up, and put him where he couldn't worry them any more."

"Maybe he'll drop out of sight," said Tom. But this was not to be. Tad Sobber was to cause a great deal of trouble, as we shall learn in the near future. The young rascal had convinced himself that the Stanhope fortune belonged to him, and he meant to leave no stone unturned to get possession of it.

CHAPTER II

THE FIRE ON THE STEAMER

"That's the way to do it!"

The cry came as Tom knocked a neat liner out to center field. He managed to get to first base with ease, while Dick, on the alert, slid to the home plate just before the ball came in.

"That gives us five runs, anyway!" was Stanley's comment. "Now, Spud, see what you can do."

"Here is where I knock one across the river and back," declared Spud Jackson, as he came forward with a bat. "Better chase your men away out," he added to Frank Holden.

"They can use nets," answered the pitcher with a grin.

Spud had a ball and a strike called on him and then met the leather and sent it to the shortstop. Tom had to run for second and he legged it with might and main. But the ball got there ahead of him and he was put out, and so was the runner at first.

"Wow!" cried Songbird. "Thought you were going to knock the ball across the river and back, Spud."

"So I did," answered Spud, as he walked up from first. "It landed on the other side, bounced back, and the shortstop got it. Fierce luck, eh?" And he cut a face that made many of the students standing by laugh outright.

In the next inning the other side added two runs to their total. One of these runs was made by Sam, much to the youngest Rover's satisfaction.

"We've got you going!" he cried, to his brothers and the others. "Might as well give up."

"Huh! we haven't started yet," retorted Tom. He turned to William Philander Tubbs, who had strolled near. "Say, Tubby, old boy, lend me your green socks for luck, will you?"

"Oh, Tom, please don't ask me to—ah—lend those socks," pleaded William Philander, innocently. "They are the only pair of that shade I have, and the young ladies say——"

"They can't resist you when you have them on," finished Tom. "All right, if you want me to lose the game, keep the socks," and the fun-loving Rover put on a mournful look.

"But, my dear Tom, how can my socks have anything to do with the game?" questioned the dude, helplessly.

"Why, it's a psychological phenomena, Tublets. Sort of an inter-mental telepathy, so to speak—a rhomboid compendium indexus, as it were. Of course you understand," said Tom, soberly.

"Why—ah—I don't think I do, Tom," stammered the dude. "But I can't loan the socks, really I can't!" And he backed away with all possible haste, while some of the students poked each other in the ribs and some laughed outright.

"Now then, here is where we go at 'em, hammer and tongs!" cried Dick, as he walked to the plate. And he met the first ball pitched and lined a beautiful three-bagger to deep center.

"Hurrah! That's the way to do it!" yelled Tom. "Leg it, old man, leg it!"

"We've struck our gait!" sang out another player. "Now, Tom, you've got to bring him home sure."

Tom was on the alert and after one strike managed to send the ball down into left field. Dick came home and the batter got to second, although it was a tight squeeze.

Spud was up next, and this time his face wore a "do-or-die" look. He had two balls called on him, and then whack! his bat struck the ball and the horsehide went sailing far over the right fielder's head.

"Say, that's a beaut!"

"Come on in, Tom!"

"Make it a two-bagger, Spud!"

"You can get to third if you try!" yelled Dick, and Spud did try and landed in a cloud of dust on third base just a second before the ball got there.

"Now then, Wilson, bring Spud in," said Dick, to the next fellow at the bat.

"Make it a homer and bring yourself in too, Wilson," added Tom.

"By chimminy! Make him two home runs while you are at it alretty!" cried Max Spangler, with a broad smile. Since arriving at Brill the German American lad had become quite a baseball "fan."

"Hi, there, you fellows!" came unexpectedly from the center fielder.

"What's the matter?" yelled back Frank Holden, stepping out of the pitcher's box and turning around.

"Something is wrong on the river."

"Wrong on the river?" queried several, in a chorus.

"Yes. Don't you hear the screaming?"

"Time!" cried the umpire, and the game came to a stop.

"Say, that is somebody screaming!" exclaimed Stanley. "Sounds like a girl's voice."

"It's from that excursion boat!" said another student. And as he spoke he pointed to a small river steamer, gaily decorated with flags and bunting, that had appeared around a bend of the stream.

"Why, that's the Thistle!" ejaculated Dick.

"The Thistle?" repeated Sam. "Oh, Dick, that's the steamer the girls from Hope were going to use for their picnic up the river!"

"I know it."

"Do you suppose Grace and Nellie and Dora are on board?"

"More than likely."

"What's the trouble?"

"They are yelling like Indians!" cried the center fielder. "Come on, something is wrong, sure!"

On the instant the game of baseball was forgotten, and like a drove of wild horses the college boys raced down to the edge of the river, which at this point was over a quarter of a mile wide but quite shallow. As they did this they heard the steam whistle of the Thistle sound out loud and long.

"That's a call for assistance, that's certain," said Dick.

"Oh, I hope the girls are safe!" murmured his youngest brother.

"She's on fire, that's what's the matter!" exclaimed Tom. "See the smoke coming from the cabin!"

"Fire! fire! fire!" was the cry taken up on all sides. "The steamer is on fire!"

"Why don't they run to the dock?" asked one of the students.

"Can't—it isn't deep enough," was the reply. "They are going to dredge out the channel this summer."

"They are turning towards shore!" came, a second later, and then it could be seen that the Thistle had turned partly around. But the next instant the vessel ran into a mud shoal and there she stuck.

"Come on, let us get out and help those who are on board!" cried Dick, and started on a run for the college boathouse, located two hundred yards further up the shore.

The alarm was now general, and fully two score of students and several of the faculty, as well as some workmen, were running for the boathouse, to get out the rowboats and other craft usually housed there.

"Stanley, how about your gasolene launch?" questioned Dick, as they raced along the river bank.

"She's all ready to use," was the answer. "I had her out a little while early this morning."

"Then I'll go out with you in that, if you say so."

"Sure," was the ready response.

"Want us?" queried Tom.

"You and Sam better bring another boat," answered Dick. "The more the better. The Thistle must have quite a crowd on board—if all the Hope students went on that picnic."

"Grace said about thirty girls were going," replied Sam. "Oh, if they get burned——"

"They won't wait for that—they'll jump into the river first," answered Tom soberly. For the time being all the fun was knocked out of him.

While talking, the boys had been busy with the boats. Stanley's gasolene launch was pushed out, and he and Dick leaped aboard, and the latter set the flywheel going. The engine was in good running order, and soon a steady put-put! sounded out, and the craft headed for the burning steamer. But, as quick as Dick and Stanley were in their movements, Tom and Sam were equally alert, and as the launch moved away Tom and his brother scrambled into a rowboat, oars in hand, and caught fast to the power craft with a boathook.

"You can pull us as well as not," said Tom.

"Right you are," answered Stanley. "And the quicker both boats get to that steamer the better."

As they drew closer to the Thistle they saw a volume of smoke roll up from the engine room. A barrel of oil had taken fire and the crew had found it impossible to subdue the conflagration. As yet the fire was only a small one, but there was no telling how soon it would spread, and the seminary girls on board were panic-stricken, more especially as the teacher who chanced to be with them was herself an extremely nervous person.

"Oh, girls, what shall we do?" asked Grace Laning, after the first dreadful alarm was at an end.

"Perhaps we had better jump overboard," suggested Nellie Laning. "I don't want to be burned alive!" And her wide-open eyes showed her terror.

"Don't jump yet," said Dora Stanhope, as bravely as she could.

"Oh, girls, we'll be burned to death! I know it, I feel it!" wailed another seminary student.

"We are near Brill College," said another. "Let us cry for help!" And then commenced the screaming that reached the players on the ball field and others near the water's edge.

In the meantime, the captain of the steamer, aided by his men, was doing all in his power to subdue the flames. But oil when on fire is a hard thing to fight. The blaze was close to the engine room, and presently both the engineer and the firemen were driven from their posts. Then the steamer became unmanageable and drifted on the mud shoal, as already mentioned.

"We'll have to get out the small boats," cried the captain. But even as he spoke he knew that the small boats were of no avail, for they had not been used since the Thistle had been put into commission, three years before, and they were dried out, and would fill with water as soon as unshipped. Life preservers were to be had, and a few of the girls were thoughtful enough to supply themselves with these.

"Crowd her, Stanley!" cried Dick, as the launch headed straight for the burning steamer.

"I'll give her all she will stand," responded the owner of the launch, and he turned the lever down another notch. The revolutions of the flywheel increased, and the water was churned up in a white foam at the stern.

"Look out, back there, that you aren't swamped!" yelled Stanley to Tom and Sam.

"We'll look out!" was Sam's answer. "Only hurry up, that's all!"

As the launch and the rowboat it was towing neared the burning steamer the college students gazed eagerly at the forms on the forward deck of the Thistle. Nearly all of the seminary girls were still screaming, and some were waving their arms wildly.

"Help! help! help!" was the cry wafted over the water.

"We are coming!" yelled Dick. "Don't jump overboard unless you are good swimmers!"

"Dick! Dick!" screamed Dora. "Oh, Dick!"

"Dora!" he answered.

"Oh, Tom!" came from Nellie. "Please take us off!"

"Sam, you are just in time!" added Grace.

"We'll get you off—don't worry!" cried Dick. "Just wait till we can bring the boats alongside and then——"

He was interrupted by a mad yell from one of the men on the steamer.

"Hurry up and leave!" yelled the man in terror. "We can't get at the boilers no more and I guess she is going to blow up!"

CHAPTER III

COLLEGE BOYS TO THE RESCUE

"Oh, Dick! do you think the steamer will really blow up?" gasped Sam, as the two small boats ranged up beside the larger vessel.

"Perhaps—if they can't get at the boilers to let off steam," was Dick's answer. "But they ought to have safety valves."

"Maybe the man is so excited he doesn't know what he is talking about," put in Tom.

Fortunately the Thistle was not a high boat, but broad and shallow, so the rail of the vessel was but a few feet above that of the launch and the rowboat.

"Come, Dora, and Nellie and Grace!" called out Dick. "We'll help you down." He turned to Stanley. "Can you hold her?"

"Sure! But what are you going to do?"

"Climb up to the rail and help them down."

"I'll do the same!" cried Tom. "Steady the rowboat, Sam!"

In a few seconds Dick and Tom were at the rail of the Thistle. All of the girls who had been out for a picnic were in a bunch, and many of them were still screaming for help. But Dora and the Laning girls were now quiet, realizing that aid was close at hand. Another gasolene launch was coming up, dragging behind it nearly every rowboat Brill possessed.

It did not take Dick long to assist Dora over the rail and into the launch, and Nellie and Grace and several other girls followed. In the meantime Sam rescued a teacher and two girls. By this time the other launch was at hand, with the additional rowboats, and in a very few minutes all of the passengers of the Thistle had been transferred. In the excitement one of the college boys and one of the seminary girls fell overboard, but the other Brill lads promptly came to the rescue.

IT DID NOT TAKE DICK LONG TO ASSIST DORA INTO THE LAUNCH.

"Let us land the girls on the shore and then try to save the steamer," suggested Dick.

"That's the talk!" cried Stanley.

"Be careful—if she is ready to blow up!" warned Spud. "I don't want to be blown into the middle of next year!"

"She won't blow up!" cried the captain, who was still trying to direct his men as to what to do. "Don't you hear the steam going off?"

"Then we'll do what we can for you," answered several of the college youths.

One after another the small boats landed on the shore, which was but a hundred yards away.

"Sam, you stay with the girls," said Dick to his youngest brother. "They may want you to do something for them."

"Oh, Dick, don't get into trouble!" begged Dora, and bent her tender eyes full upon him.

"Don't worry, Dora."

"And, Tom, you be careful, too," added Nellie.

"I will, Nellie," he answered.

Both of the gasolene launches, with eight of the college boys on board, returned to the Thistle. The thick smoke of the burning oil was still rolling up the companionways and hatchways. But, with the deck cleared of passengers, the crew had a better chance to fight the flames.

"Captain, what can we do?" demanded Dick, as he climbed on deck, followed by Stanley and by Allen Charter, who owned the second launch.

"I don't know," answered the master of the vessel, almost helplessly. "That oil burns like fury."

"Wouldn't sand be good for the flames?" questioned Allen.

"Yes—but I ain't got none—that is, not more'n a shovelful or two."

"There is sand up at the boat dock!" cried Stanley. "They are going to use it for the new garage foundation."

"Maybe we can haul the steamer up there," suggested another student.

"We can try it," answered Allen Charter. "What do you say, Captain?"

"I'm willing—if you can budge her."

"She can't be stuck very fast," said Tom.

The college boys got into the two launches once more, and as speedily as possible ropes were fastened to the Thistle. Then the launches were started up and all power was turned on. At first the big vessel refused to budge.

"Don't seem to be making any headway," observed Frank Holden.

"Here we go!" cried Dick, and he was right. Slowly the Thistle moved off the mud shoal and commenced to turn. Then as slowly the vessel followed the two launches in the direction of the dock.

"We want sand!" yelled some of the boys on board. "Get the sand ready!"

The cries were understood, and by the time the Thistle was brought close to the dock, fully a score of boys stood ready with boxes and pails of sand to come on board. A gangplank was thrown out, and on deck hurried the sand carriers.

"That's the stuff!" cried the captain, and his face brightened with hope. "Just give that sand to me and the engineer. We know where to put it."

Boxes and pails were passed over with great rapidity, and the sand was taken below and thrown on the burning oil. It was hard and dangerous work and some of the men were all but overcome. While the work was going on Doctor Wallington arrived, followed by the college janitor and some others, all carrying fire extinguishers.

"Here, use these!" cried the master of the institution, and the fire extinguishers were soon brought into play. Dick got one and Tom another and with them succeeded in putting out the flames that had reached one end of the cabin.

All of the men and the boys worked like Trojans, and before long it could be seen that they were getting the best of the conflagration. The smoke was growing thinner and only an occasional spurt of flames showed itself.

"Hurrah! we'll have it out soon!" cried Tom, enthusiastically.

"Yes, and I'll be mighty glad of it," muttered the captain of the vessel.

"I hope you are insured, Captain," said Dick.

"I am—but a fire is always a loss, anyhow."

"That is true."

The boys and the men continued their labors, and inside of half an hour the fire was under control. Some of the men went below to make an examination.

"It's mostly around the boilers," said the engineer. "It's a great mess."

The hands of the Thistle continued to labor and in a short while the last spark of fire was put out. Then a tug was telephoned for to tow the vessel down the river to the town.

In the meanwhile Dick and Tom rejoined their brother and the girls. The students from Hope, with their teacher, had been invited to make themselves at home in the reception rooms of the college, and word of the disaster to the Thistle had been telephoned to the seminary. Word was also sent to the town, and a large number of persons came out to learn the extent of the disaster.

"The newspapers will make a spread of this," was Tom's comment. "We'd better send word home that everybody is safe."

"Yes, do!" cried Nellie. "Mamma will be so worried when she hears about it."

"Yes, we must send word at once," added Dora. "Mamma can't stand any excitement. She has had more than enough lately."

"You mean because of this affair about the fortune, I suppose," returned Dick. "It was an outrage for Tad Sobber to hold up the money the way he did."

"Yes, Dick, but that is not all," answered Dora. "I was going to tell you of something else the first chance I got." She looked around, to see if anybody else was listening.

"About what, Dora?" he questioned, quickly.

"About old Josiah Crabtree."

"Crabtree!" exclaimed the eldest Rover boy in astonishment. "What about him."

The person mentioned will be well remembered by my old readers. Josiah Crabtree had once been a teacher at Putnam Hall and had caused the Rover boys a good deal of trouble. When Crabtree had discovered that the widow Stanhope was holding some money in trust for Dora, and also had quite some money of her own, he had done his best to get the widow to marry him. At that time Mrs. Stanhope had been sickly and easily led, and Crabtree had exercised a sort of hypnotic influence over her and all but forced her into a marriage. But his plot had been thwarted by the Rovers, and later on, Josiah Crabtree had been caught doing something that was against the law and had been sent to prison for it.

"He has been bothering mamma again," went on Dora.

"Been bothering your mother! How can that be, since he is in prison?"

"He is out again. It seems that while he was in prison he acted so well that some folks took pity on him and got up a petition to have him pardoned. Now he is out, and almost the first thing he did was to call on mamma."

"What did he have to say?"

"I don't know, exactly. But I do know that mamma was greatly frightened, almost as much so as when Tad Sobber called and said he was going to get the fortune."

"Did your mother think that Crabtree had reformed?"

"She wasn't sure about that. What scared her was the fact that he called at all. She expected never to see him again."

"Why didn't she order him to keep away? That is what she ought to do."

"I know it. But you know how mamma is, rather weak and not wanting to make trouble for anybody. She said she wished he wouldn't call again, and she was greatly upset."

"Then it's a good thing you are going home soon, Dora. You'll have to stay with her this summer."

"Yes, we and the Lanings are going to stay altogether."

"I wish we were going off on another trip together, Dora," said Dick, in a lower voice. "Wasn't our trip to Treasure Isle great?"

"Perfectly lovely—in spite of the troubles we had," answered the girl.

"That's the kind of a trip I am going to take again—when we go off on our honeymoon, Dora."

"Oh, Dick!" And Dora flushed prettily. "How can you say such things, and in a crowd! Somebody may hear you!"

"Oh, I only want you to know——" began Dick, but just then Tom and Sam brushed up with Nellie and Grace, so the sentence was not finished. Dora gave him a meaning look and he held her arm considerably tighter than was necessary.

"Well, the picnic is off, and they are going to tow the steamer back," explained Tom.

"And the young ladies are to be taken back to the seminary in the college carryall and carriages," added Sam.

"What a shame!" murmured Tom innocently. "Now they are here I thought they'd stay till we went home."

"Tom Rover! what an idea!" shrieked Nellie. "Why, we've got to go back for our last examination, and to pack."

"Remember, we are to go East on the same train," warned Dick. "Let me know just when you can start and I'll arrange for the tickets."

"We are to leave Hope on Wednesday," said Grace.

"That will suit us," answered Tom. "We might leave Tuesday afternoon, but it won't hurt to stay here one night more."

"It will give us time to rest up from the last day's fun," added Dick.

"Do you expect any fun on the last day?" questioned Dora.

"Do we?" cried Tom. "Just you wait and see, that's all! We'll turn old Brill inside out and upside down!" he added, with emphasis.

CHAPTER IV

WHAT FLOCKLEY HAD TO TELL

It was not long before the carryall of the college and several carriages were brought into use and in these the girls and their teacher were placed.

"We'll see you Sunday!" called out Dick to Dora.

"Yes, we might as well go to church together," added Sam; and so it was arranged.

"But about those messages home?" asked Nellie.

"We'll send 'em—don't you worry," answered Tom. "We'll go right down to Ashton now—on our bicycles." And then the turnouts rolled away, and the students of Brill were left once more to themselves.

"Well, those girls can be thankful that the fire was no worse," was Stanley's comment.

"I reckon they are thankful," answered Dick.

"They were mighty glad we came up with the boats," said another student. "Some of them thanked us over and over again."

"Huh! I don't think the boats were needed," muttered Dudd Flockley. "The water isn't over two feet deep. They could have waded ashore."

"The water is four to six feet deep and the bottom out there is soft mud!" cried Tom, "They'd either have to swim or run the risk of getting stuck in the mud!"

"Oh, Dudd is sore—because his hat was mashed," cried another pupil.

"He's sore because none of the girls thanked him," added another.

"And he wasn't thanked because he didn't do anything," said Spud.

"Aw! give us a rest!" muttered Flockley, and then walked away without another word.

"Say, did anybody notice William Philander Tubbs?" queried Will Faley. "He didn't do much towards rescuing the girls, but when they got ashore he ran all the way to the college to get a whisk broom, to brush them off!"

"Hurrah for Washtub! He's the real hero!" cried Tom. "He thinks of the truly important things!"

"It was a grand spectacle—the thick black smoke pouring from that steamer," came from Songbird. "I—er—I helped to get the sand. But even as I worked I couldn't help but make up a few lines. They run like this:"

> "All wrapt in flames, behold our craft!
> She'll plough the main no more!
> Her gallant crew may well shed tears——"

"She's burnt out to the core!"

finished Tom. "Only that isn't true, for the Thistle wasn't burnt to the core—in fact, the captain says she was burnt very little—thanks to the unswerving devotion of the gallant band of Brill fire-fighters who, undaunted by the terrifying perils of the horrible occasion succeeded, after almost superhuman endeavors, in quelling——"

"Great hambones! Tom's sprung a leak!" interrupted Sam. "Tom, put on your low speed, or you'll run away with yourself."

"Ha, wretch! to interrupt such a superb flow of oratory!" cried the fun-loving Rover, in assumed grieved tones.

"As if you didn't interrupt my poetry," came ruefully from Songbird. "The next time I—er—recite I'll see to it that you are not around."

"Don't do it, Birdie, I beg of you. I wouldn't miss your verses for a quart of freckles."

"Ashton—and the telegraph office!" sang out Dick. "Who is going along?" And the touch of hard feelings between Tom and Songbird was forgotten. Tom knew he had no right to interrupt the would-be poet the way he did, but—well, Tom was Tom, and he couldn't help it.

The matter was talked over, and a party of nine was made up, including the Rovers and Songbird and Stanley. Soon the lads were on the way, having received permission from Doctor Wallington to be a little late for supper.

"We'll return home by the Carlip Road," said Dick.

"Right you are," added Tom. He knew this would please Songbird, for the route mentioned would take them past the Sanderson farm, and the would-be poet would have a chance to see Minnie, the farmer's daughter, with whom Songbird had of late been quite smitten.

The messages for the Lanings and Mrs. Stanhope were soon despatched, and the Rovers also sent word to their folks, saying when they might be expected home. Then the crowd divided, and Tom, Dick, Sam and Songbird took to the road leading past the Sanderson cottage.

"Remember how we pitched into Flockley and Koswell here?" remarked Sam, as the farm came into view.

"Indeed I do," answered Dick. He turned to Songbird. "You can ride ahead if you wish. We'll go on slowly."

"All right," answered the other. "I won't be long. I only want to leave a volume of 'Poems of Love' I picked up in a bookstore yesterday," and away Songbird pedaled towards the Sanderson house.

"He's got 'em sure," said Sam, with a grin. "Well, Minnie is a nice girl."

"Huh! I suppose Songbird has as much right to be soft on her as you have to be soft on Grace!" was Tom's blunt comment.

"Not to mention you and Nellie," retorted his younger brother.

The three Rovers rode past the house and then stopped to rest under a wide-spreading tree. Some June apples were handy, and they munched on these until Songbird reappeared, about a quarter of an hour later.

"Say, it took more than two minutes to deliver that book," remarked Dick. "We were just getting ready to go on without you."

"Don't forget we want some supper," added Sam.

"I—er—I just stopped to point out several poems of special interest," explained Songbird. "One was on 'Her Eyes So Blue and True.' It's a grand poem, and——"

"Let me see, Miss Sanderson's eyes are blue, aren't they?" questioned Sam, gravely.

"I wasn't speaking of her eyes—I meant the poem's—that is—those spoken of in the poem," stammered Songbird. "By the way," he added, hastily, to hide his confusion, "I just heard strange news. Minnie and her father were down in Ashton a couple of days ago and they saw Dudd Flockley at the depot, and he was talking with Jerry Koswell and Bart Larkspur."

"Koswell and Larkspur!" exclaimed Dick. "I didn't think they would dare to show themselves around here."

"Just what I thought, but Mr. Sanderson and Minnie were both sure they saw the pair. They were talking very earnestly to Flockley, as if trying to get him to do something, and Minnie says Flockley said, 'I'll see about it—maybe I can go.'"

"Humph! Flockley promised that he would drop Koswell and Larkspur," said Sam.

"He'd better—if he knows where he is well off," added Tom.

"What became of Koswell and Larkspur?" questioned Dick.

"Minnie says they took the night train for the East."

"The through train?"

"Yes."

"Well, then they must be a good many miles from Ashton—and I am glad of it."

"Speaking of Flockley puts me in mind of one thing—I mustn't forget to pay for that hat I smashed," said Tom.

"Better see him tonight and settle up," said Dick. "And I'll go with you. I want to speak to Flockley," he added, thoughtfully.

When the boys returned to the college they found their classmates just finishing supper. Professor Blackie looked at them rather severely, but Sam explained that they had permission from the Head to be late, so nothing was said further.

From one of the other students Dick and Sam learned that Flockley had gone for a walk behind the gymnasium, where a path led to the river. As soon as they had finished eating Tom got some money, and he and his brother set off to find the dudish student.

"There he is!" cried Dick, after quite a long walk, and he pointed to Dudd Flockley, seated on a rustic bench, smoking a cigarette. The student was alone, and looked to be in a thoughtful mood.

"Flockley, I want to settle with you for that hat," said Tom, as he came up. "And let me tell you honestly that I am sorry I mashed it."

"I think you did it on purpose," grumbled the dudish student. "You Rovers think you can do just as you please at Brill. I suppose you'll feel more important than ever—after that affair of the burning steamer," he added, bitterly.

"Dudd, let Tom pay you for the hat and then let me talk to you," said Dick, quietly. "How much did it cost?"

"Five dollars."

"Here you are then," came from Tom, and he passed over a five-dollar bill. "I didn't mash it on purpose, no matter what you think."

"All right—have your own way about it, Rover," and Dudd pocketed the bill carelessly.

"Dudd, you met Koswell and Larkspur the other day," went on Dick, sitting down on the rustic bench.

"Did Minnie Sanderson tell you that?"

"She told Songbird Powell and he told us."

"Well, what of it? They came to Ashton on business—they had to get their stuff away from the college."

"Did you meet them by accident?"

"What business is that of yours?" And Dudd Flockley's voice grew aggressive.

"Perhaps it is none of my business, Dudd. But, just the same, I am going to talk to you about it. You know all about what happened in the past. Koswell and Larkspur are bad eggs—and if they can drag you down with them they will do it. Now, you promised to turn over a new leaf and on the strength of that we went to Doctor Wallington and persuaded him to give you another chance. It isn't fair for you to go back on your word, and take up with Koswell and Larkspur again."

"Are you going to tell the doctor that I met them?" asked Flockley, in alarm.

"No—at least, not for the present. But I want you to promise to drop that pair."

"I have dropped them—that is, as much as I can."

"Then why do you meet them?"

"I'll tell you why!" burst out the dudish student, bitterly. "Because I can't drop them altogether. They know everything of what happened as well as I do, and they said if I dropped them entirely—refused to help them—they would expose me to the whole world! If they should tell my folks——" Flockley did not finish, but his head sunk on his breast, and Dick and Tom understood.

"It's too bad—a burning shame!" murmured Tom. "Flockley, I am sorry from the bottom of my heart!"

"I don't think I would take their threats too seriously," said Dick. "They are down and out, and, of course, very bitter. But they don't dare to come out against you openly."

"Yes—but they can do a whole lot of things behind my back!" groaned Dudd Flockley. "Oh, you don't know what I have suffered since Jerry and Bart ran away! They have written me letters, and they have demanded money——"

"Demanded money. Then they are blackmailers, Dudd!"

"Oh, they said I owed them the money on bets. But I didn't—at least, I don't think I did. But I had to give up. At the depot that day I gave them thirty dollars—all I could scrape up."

"Where did they go to?"

"To New York, and from there they are going to Boston and then to some place off the coast of Maine."

"And they wanted you to join them?"

"Yes."

"Don't you do it!" cried Dick, earnestly. "Don't you do it, Dudd! Wash your hands of them and refuse to have anything more to do with them."

"I will—if I can," murmured Dudd Flockley. And then, as some other students approached, the talk had to come to an end.

CHAPTER V

A CELEBRATION ON THE CAMPUS

"Say, Tom, this is great!"

"What now, Sam?"

"All of us have passed the exams with credit marks."

"All of us? Are you sure?"

"Yes, I was in the classroom not five minutes ago and got the good word."

"Say, that makes me feel like dancing a jig!" cried Tom Rover, and he did a few steps on the floor of the gymnasium. "Won't the folks at home be tickled when they hear of it!"

"Dick got the highest marks of the class," went on the youngest Rover. "Stanley is next."

"Where do we come in?"

"You are seventh."

"Oh, lucky seventh!" murmured the fun-loving Rover. "It's always that way! At baseball if I do anything at all it is usually in the seventh innings."

"Don't grow superstitious, Tom."

"Where do you come in?"

"I stand fifth."

"That's splendid, Sam! Oh, come on and jig!" And Tom caught his brother by the waist and whirled him around. Over the gymnasium floor they went, to land suddenly into the form of William Philander Tubbs, who had just entered.

"Oh, I say, don't you know——" spluttered William Philander. He had the breath all but knocked out of his body.

"Excuse me, Tublets," cried Tom.

"Don't call me Tublets, please," expostulated the tall student. "And please don't run into me again."

"Oh, Sam and I were only doing a war dance," cried Tom, gaily. "We have passed our exams."

"You are very rude, don't you know."

"It shan't occur again, Philliam Willander."

"William Philander, Tom."

"To be sure, I am glad I am sorry that I remember I forgot," answered Tom, gravely. "It shan't occur again the last time, I assure you."

"Oh, Tom, let up!" put in Dick, who had come up. "We have passed—doesn't that make you feel good?"

"And you at the head of the class, Dick! Say, if I had wings, or an aeroplane, I'd fly!"

"Come on for a last swing on the rings!" exclaimed Dick, and led the way, and soon all of the brothers were exercising on the flying rings with which the college gymnasium was equipped.

It was Monday afternoon and studies were practically at an end and all the boys had to do was to pack up their things and wait for the time to go home.

On Sunday morning the three Rovers had driven over to Hope Seminary and taken Dora and the Lanings to church. At that time it had been arranged that all should start for home on the early morning train on the following Wednesday. They would travel together as far as a place called Cartown and then separate, the girls to go on to Cedarville and the lads to journey to Oak Run, the nearest railroad station to the farm.

"Some of the fellows are going home Tuesday night," said Dick. "So if we are going to have any fun we had better have it Monday night," and so it was arranged.

The Rovers had had no further opportunity to talk to Dudd Flockley. They noticed that Flockley avoided them and seemed to be in deep thought.

"I suppose he is thinking of Koswell and Larkspur," said Dick. "Poor fellow, I feel sorry for him! I hope he doesn't let them drag him down any deeper."

"He has only himself to blame for the position he is in," said Sam. "We did what we could for him—more than most fellows would do, Dick."

"That is true, Sam."

Supper was had at the usual hour and then the students commenced to gather on the campus and down by the river. Nearly everybody was in good humor, and they sang, and made a racket generally. Bonfires were lit, and also a string of paper lanterns.

"I've got a surprise for the crowd," said Tom to Sam. "Come on and help me to wake Brill up."

"How?" questioned the younger Rover.

"I'll soon show you—come with me."

Tom led the way to a storeroom behind the gymnasium. In one corner, under some old canvas, was a box several feet long, that had come in by express.

"I had the time of my life getting this here without having it pass inspection by the Head," said Tom.

"What's in it, Tom?"

"Fireworks—a regular Fourth of July outfit—rockets, Roman candles, pinwheels, bombs, and all. I sent the order to the city a week ago."

"Good for you!" cried Sam, with a grin. "This will certainly wake up the natives."

"See if you can get Dick to help us. But be careful—I want to surprise all the rest, even Stanley."

"I'll get him," answered Sam, and hurried off.

A little later, when it was quite dark, the three Rover boys shouldered the big box and carried it to the edge of the woods beside the campus. Then they opened the box and took out the fireworks.

"Guess we'll send up a few bombs first, just to wake everybody up," said Tom.

A minute later a large-sized bomb went whistling upward in the air. It flew high over the college building, to burst with a deafening report.

"Hello, what's that?" yelled several.

"Who fired that shot?"

"Did a cannon go off?"

"It was an aerial bomb—and there goes another!" cried Allen Charter. "Somebody is celebrating in earnest."

All of the students on the campus stared at the bombs in wonder, while others came rushing from various buildings, to learn the meaning of the reports.

"Who shot off the cannon?" stormed Professor Sharp. "It's against the rules to shoot off that cannon without permission."

"It wasn't the cannon, Professor," explained Frank Holden. "It was a bomb. Somebody——"

Boom! went another bomb, and it was right over the professor's head. The professor was scared and ducked wildly.

"I want the person who is doing that——" he commenced, but got no further, for just then a big rocket went hissing through the air, to burst a second later and let fall a beautiful shower of golden rain.

"Oh, isn't that grand!"

"Say, this is something like!"

"Must be that Doctor Wallington meant to surprise us."

Far into the sky flew two more rockets, one letting fall some chains of red, white and blue and the other some strange fish-like shapes that darted hither and thither.

"This is certainly all to the merry!" murmured Stanley. "It's as good as a Fourth of July exhibition."

"Look at the Roman candles!" cried Max, pointing over to the woods. From among the trees three large Roman candles were sending their balls of various colors high into the air.

"This is a surprise and no mistake," murmured Doctor Wallington, as he gazed at the fireworks.

"Didn't you know about them, Doctor?" questioned Allen Charter.

"No. It must be the work of some students."

"I'm going to see who is doing it!" cried Stanley, and ran for the woods, followed by a score of others.

When the crowd arrived they found Dick, Tom and Sam in the act of setting off more rockets and Roman candles.

"Say, you sure surprised us!" cried Stanley.

"It's out of sight!" murmured Spud.

"Huh! I am sorry," murmured Tom. "I thought it was very much in sight."

"Oh, you know what I mean, Tom. It's bang-up."

"It sure is that!" cried Sam, as one of the rockets exploded with a loud report.

"Here are some packages of red lights," said Tom. "I want every fellow here to take one and light it. Then we'll form a procession and march around the buildings."

"That's the talk!" cried Stanley. "Say, if we only had a band!"

"I'll go and git my drum," cried Max, who chanced to own one.

"And I'll get my bugle," added a student who possessed such an instrument.

By the time the drum and bugle were brought the red lights were lit, and amid a general cheering the students got into line and the march around the college buildings began.

"Come on in, Dudd!" cried Dick, to Flockley, who stood looking on, and he passed over a red light which the student took rather unwillingly. "Everybody in this march!"

Around and around the buildings marched the students. William Philander Tubbs wanted to keep out of the procession, but he was caught by Sam and Tom and made to carry a flag consisting of an old red sweater tied to the handle of a broom. Other boys carried the college colors, and they added to the din with tin horns and wooden rattles.

"My! but this is disgraceful!" muttered Professor Sharp, in disgust.

"Disgraceful?" cried Doctor Wallington. "Not at all, sir. Let the young men enjoy themselves. They are doing no harm."

"I don't like so much noise," snapped Asa Sharp, and retired to the college building.

"I've got about a dozen packs of firecrackers," said Tom, a little later. "We mustn't forget to shoot them off."

"Pass 'em around, Tom!" cried Stanley, and the firecrackers were quickly distributed.

"Come on and give old Filbury a scare," suggested Spud, and before anybody could stop him he went off after the old man who worked around the dormitories. He found Filbury on a step-ladder, fixing a lamp, and he very quietly pinned his firecrackers to the old man's coat tail.

"What do you want, sir?" asked the old man, as he started to come down the step-ladder.

"I wanted to ask you if you knew where my baseball was," asked Spud, innocently.

"No, I don't know nuthing about baseballs," growled Filbury. He sniffed the air. "Say, smells like something burning around here!" he cried. "Did any of them fireworks set fire to the buildings?"

"I guess not," answered Spud. "But about that ball——"

Crack! bang! crack! went a number of the firecrackers and poor Filbury leaped several feet into the air. Then he turned hastily around.

"What are you doing?" he demanded, and then a long string of the firecrackers went off, causing him to whirl first to one side and then another. He put his hands behind him. "Ouch! I'm burnt!" he screamed.

"Whoopla! that's the way to celebrate!" roared Spud. "Nothing like having fun while you are at it!"

"I'll 'fun' you!" yelled Filbury, in anger, and of a sudden he drew off his coat and commenced to chase Spud. Down the corridor went the pair. And then Filbury cast the coat with the firecrackers still exploding, at Spud's head.

Spud ducked and the coat sailed over his head, to enter a doorway that was partly open. Then another person appeared. It was Professor Asa Sharp. He stepped on the coat and as he did so several of the firecrackers went off, one hitting him directly in the chin.

"Oh!" he screamed. "I am hit! Take those fireworks away!" And he bolted down the hallway with all the speed he could command. He ran out on a porch and then down on the campus, where Tom and Sam were bending over something on the ground.

"Look out! Run!" yelled Tom, and then he and his brother leaped back. In bewilderment Professor Asa Sharp stood still. Then a terrific explosion rent the air, and a great shower of sparks flew in all directions.

CHAPTER VI

GOOD-BYE TO BRILL

"Say, that was an explosion!"

"Who was that stood so close?"

"Was he hurt?"

These and a number of other cries and questions came from the students of Brill who had witnessed the setting off, by Tom and Sam, of the last of the fireworks.

As for the two Rover boys, they knew not what to say. Both stared helplessly for a moment at Professor Sharp.

"Hi! hi!" spluttered that individual. "Stop it! Do you want to blow me to pieces? Oh, I'm all on fire!" And, seeing that his coat had ignited from some of the sparks, he commenced to dance around in terror.

"Here—wait, Professor!" called out Tom. "Let me knock out that fire!" And he began to beat out the flames with his hands.

"Don't—don't hit me so hard, Rover!" snarled the professor, for in his excitement Tom was pounding away harder than intended. Sam also came forward to put out the sparks, and so did Dick and some others.

"Here, give me that broom, Tubbs!" cried the eldest Rover, and catching the article, Dick whipped off the red sweater and then used the broom to sweep from Asa Sharp what was left of the fire.

In a few seconds more the danger was over. In the meanwhile a big crowd commenced to collect around the instructor and those who had set off the fireworks.

"This is an outrage!" fumed Professor Sharp. "An outrage! I'll have the law on you for it!" And he glared savagely at Tom and Sam.

"I don't see how you can blame us, sir," answered Tom, stoutly. "We were just setting off the fireworks when you ran right into the midst of them."

"Nonsense! nonsense! You did it on purpose!"

"You certainly ran right into the things, just as we had lit them," said Sam. "I don't see how you can blame us for that."

"You'll see! I shall report to Doctor Wallington at once!" stormed Asa Sharp, and hurried off with his face drawn down in sour determination.

"Phew! I guess we are in hot water, Tom!" whispered Sam.

"I don't see how he can blame us, Sam."

"Well, in one way, we had no right to set off the fireworks."

"Indeed! And why not, on the last day of the term, I'd like to know? The doctor saw us, and he didn't say anything about stopping."

"I really think it was Professor Sharp's fault," said Allen Charter, who had been standing near. "He certainly ran right into the midst of the lighted fireworks. I saw him do it."

"Will you say a word for us, Charter, if we are reported to the Head?" asked Tom.

"Certainly."

"And so will I," added Stanley.

"And I—if you won't make me carry that horrid broom any longer," lisped William Philander Tubbs.

"Say, I guess I'm as much to blame as anybody!" came from Spud, who had followed Asa Sharp from the college building. And then he told of what had happened between himself, Filbury and the instructor.

"I doubt if you hear any more about it," said Charter. And he was practically right. The subject was barely mentioned by Doctor Wallington, and neither Tom nor Sam were censured for what had occurred. And that was fair, for the Rover boys had really not been to blame.

Later in the evening the college boys had something of a feast. A number had "chipped in" and bought some soda water, ginger ale, ice-cream and cake in Ashton, and the improvised feast was held in the boathouse, which was strung with lanterns. Several of the students made speeches, others sang, and Songbird was called on to recite an original poem, a request that pleased him greatly.

"Say, boys, Brill is a great place after all!" remarked Dick, when he and his brothers were retiring for the night "At first I thought I shouldn't like it quite as well as dear old Putnam Hall, but I am gradually changing my mind."

"This place grows on one," returned Tom. "I suppose by the time we finish up here we'll hate to leave, just as we hated to leave old Putnam."

"Well, we won't be college boys so very long," remarked Sam. "Almost before you know it, we'll be men and out in the world of business."

"And settled down, maybe, with a family of children to support," added Tom, with a grin.

After the strenuous times of the evening before, the Rovers were glad to take it easy on Tuesday. They finished the last of their packing and Tom played a last joke on William Philander Tubbs by placing in the trunk of the fastidious student a pair of old overalls and three old farm hats found in the barn of Brill. They were hidden in the middle of the dude's things, and he locked up the trunk without discovering them.

"I hope he unpacks that trunk when the ladies are around," said Tom. "Then he can show 'em how he used to play farm hand, and wear three big straw hats at a time."

"It's too bad to part!" sighed Songbird. "Wish we were all going on another treasure hunt!" And then he commenced to warble softly:

> "I love to sail the briny deep!
> The briny deep for me!
> I love to watch the sunlit waves
> That brighten up the sea!
> I love to listen to the wind
> That fills the snowy sails!
> I love to roam around the deck——"
> "And eat the fishes' tails!"

interrupted Tom. And then he went on:

> "I love to swim upon the sand,
> And dance upon the brine,
> And write my name in salty waves,
> And hope for dinner time
> To come, so I can eat my fill
> Of sea-foam snaps and cream;
> And stand upon the quarter-deck
> A halfback of the team!"

"Humph! do you call that poetry?" snorted Songbird. "It sounds as much like it as a dog's bark sounds like a hymn!"

"Well, it would be a 'him' if he was a gentleman dog!" retorted Tom, and then Songbird turned away in momentary disgust. But soon his good humor returned and Tom and the others allowed him to "spout poetry" to his heart's content.

It had been arranged that the Rovers, Dora, and the Laning girls should meet at the Ashton depot, and it is needless to say that the three boys were on time. They were alone, for Songbird and Stanley and some of their other chums were going to take different trains.

"Don't forget to let me hear from you this summer!" said Songbird, on parting.

"Oh, we'll be sure to write," answered Dick. "Come and see me—if you get anywhere near my home," said Stanley.

"We'll remember that," returned Tom.

The boys were taken to Ashton depot in an automobile belonging to the college. Their trunks and dress-suit cases had preceded them, and as soon as they arrived they had their baggage checked straight through to Oak Run.

"I see the girls' trunks," announced Sam, who had been looking the pile of baggage over. "We could get them checked, too, if we had their tickets."

"Wonder where the girls are?" came from Tom, as he looked at his watch.

"How much time, Tom?"

"Ten minutes yet—and this train will most likely be late."

Rather impatiently the Rover boys walked up and down the platform. Presently they saw one of the Hope carryalls coming and went to meet it.

"They aren't in that," cried Sam, disappointedly.

"Another carriage coming from Hope?" queried Tom, of the carryall driver.

"Two of 'em," was the reply.

The second carriage arrived a minute later. It contained six girls and among them was Grace.

"Dora and Nellie are in the last carriage," announced the younger Laning girl. "I came on ahead to get the trunks and bags checked."

"We'll do that," answered Sam promptly. "Got the railroad tickets?"

"Yes, here they are," and Grace handed the tickets over.

It took several minutes to check the baggage, for the agent was busy, and all of the Rovers gave a hand in shifting the heavy trunks out to a place close to the tracks. Then Dick looked at his watch.

"Time for the train now," he announced. "Wonder why that carriage doesn't get here?"

"Dick is getting nervous," said Sam, with a wink.

"Oh, you are all right—with Grace here," retorted his brother.

Tom had gone up to a bend of the road to take a look. Now he came back with a shrug of his shoulders.

"Nothing but a farm wagon in sight," he announced. "And the horses are kicking up such a dust I can't see behind it."

"Oh, Tom, is it time for the train?" asked Grace, anxiously.

"It's three minutes past the time," answered Dick.

"Maybe the train is a good deal late," said Sam, hopefully. "I'll ask the agent."

He went off and in the meantime the others continued to watch the country road leading to the railroad station. All they could see was a cloud of dust that betokened the coming of a big farm wagon, on the front seat of which sat an old farmer.

"The train is coming!" cried Sam in dismay, on returning. "The agent says it will be here in about two minutes."

"Two minutes!" burst out Dick and Tom.

"Oh, they'll get left!" moaned Grace. "What shall we do? I can't go home alone! And I've got their tickets!"

"Perhaps the agent will hold the train a bit," suggested Dick.

"I hear the train now!" cried Sam, as a distant whistle sounded through the air. A moment later they saw the cars, making a broad curve around the distant hills.

Dick ran to the man who sold tickets and looked after the baggage.

"Say, we are waiting for some more passengers—some young ladies from Hope Seminary," he explained. "Can't you hold the train till they come?"

"Not much!" was the sharp answer. "The train is late already, and orders are to make as short a stop as possible."

"They are coming!" yelled Tom. "I see them away down the road!"

"Oh, call to them to hurry!" burst out Grace.

"They can't hear me," answered Tom. "They are coming as fast as the team can go."

"Won't you hold the train just a couple of minutes?" pleaded Dick.

"No, sir!" And the agent spoke with a positive snap in his voice.

Dick looked across the tracks. The farm wagon had come up, and on the seat he recognized the fat and jolly Mr. Sanderson, the father of the girl they had once saved from the annoyances of Dudd Flockley and Jerry Koswell.

"I'll get Mr. Sanderson to do the trick for me!" he muttered to himself, and ran to where the farm wagon had come to a halt.

CHAPTER VII

DREAMS OF YOUTH

"Mr. Sanderson!"

"Why, if it ain't Mr. Rover!" cried the old farmer. "Glad to see ye! Bound fer hum, I suppose?"

"Yes." Dick stepped close to the old farmer's side. "Mr. Sanderson do you want to do me a great big favor and do it quick?" he went on, earnestly.

"O' course. Wot is it?"

"Do you see that train coming?"

"Well, as my eyesight is putty good, I do," and the old farmer chuckled.

"And do you see that carriage on the road?"

"Yes—it's one of them turnouts from the gals' school."

"Some of our friends are in that carriage and I want to hold that train till they get here," continued Dick, quickly. "The station agent won't hold the train for me—so I want you to do it."

"Me? I ain't got nuthin' to do with the railroad."

"I know that. But you can hold the train, nevertheless. The train will stop just below this crossing—it always does. When it is about ready to start you drive on the track—and then your horse balks, see? You try to start him but he won't start. You fuss and pull, but the horse don't budge until those young ladies are on the train."

"By gum! I'll do it!" exclaimed the fat farmer, with a twinkle in his eyes. "This hoss is jest the one to balk, too."

"I can depend on you?"

"You kin, Mr. Rover."

"Thank you a thousand times!" returned Dick; and then he went off to rejoin his brothers and Grace.

The train had already rolled in and passengers were getting off and on, and the agent was loading on the trunks and handbags.

"Oh, if they would only hurry!" cried Grace.

"You can get aboard," said Dick. "This train won't leave just yet."

"But it is going to go before they get here," declared Sam. "It's a shame! Two minutes more would fix it—and they could hold the train as well as not."

"All aboard!" sang out the conductor, as the last of the baggage disappeared into the baggage car.

Dick looked ahead. Mr. Sanderson's farm wagon had just started to cross the tracks. He was sawing on the reins and the horse was acting in a strange manner, not knowing what to make of it. He turned part way around and faced the locomotive.

"G'lang!" sang out the old farmer. "Consarn ye! What's the matter of ye, Franky?"

"Oh, Dick, he'll be killed!" burst out Sam, in horror.

"Looks as if the horse wanted to climb over the engine," came from Tom.

"It's all right," answered the elder Rover boy in a whisper. "The engineer sees him and won't start the train. Mr. Sanderson is doing it on purpose."

"On purpose?" came from Sam and Tom, and then of a sudden they understood, and both had to turn away to hide the grins that broke out on their faces.

"Go ahead!" cried the conductor, and then he saw the trouble and ran forward to watch proceedings.

From the antics of the horse in front of the locomotive, the Rover boys turned their attention to the carriage that was approaching. As it came closer they saw Dora and Nellie waving their hands frantically.

"Wait! Wait for us!" cried out Dora, and as the carriage came to a stop she leaped out, followed by Nellie and the other girl students.

"Just in time!" sang out Dick, loudly. "Come on, here is our car!"

"Oh, what made you so late?" asked Grace. "We have been worried to death about you."

"One of the girls forgot her pocketbook and we had to drive back for it," explained Nellie. "Oh, we thought sure we would miss the train, when we saw it stop. We were so far off."

"I'll explain why you caught it later on," whispered Dick. "Now excuse me a moment," and he ran towards the locomotive.

A crowd had commenced to collect, and several folks were offering Mr. Sanderson advice. But though he seemed to try his best, his horse and wagon remained in front of the train.

"Here, let me aid you, Mr. Sanderson," cried Dick, and gave the farmer the wink. "It's all right," he added, in a whisper. "I'm your friend for life after this."

"Glad to be of service," answered the old farmer, in an equally low tone. "G'lang, Franky!" he roared suddenly, and touched the horse with his whip. At once the animal turned partly around and ran off the tracks and down the country road as if nothing out of the ordinary had happened.

"Confound that fool nag!" muttered the conductor of the train, as he consulted his watch. "Here we've lost six minutes more. Tom, can you make it up?"

"I can try," answered the engineer.

"All right! Let her go!" And Dick and the other passengers who had gone forward hopped on the train in a hurry, and the conductor followed. The train official did not suspect that the "blockading" had been done purposely, and Dick did not enlighten him.

The Rovers had secured seats for the girls and themselves in one of the parlor cars, and all were together. As the train rolled onward Dick related the particulars of the trick that had been played with the aid of Mr. Sanderson.

"Oh, Dick, how could you think of such a thing?" cried Dora.

"Oh, it just popped into my mind," he answered. "And Mr. Sanderson acted his part to perfection. Aren't you glad we did something to hold the train?"

"Indeed yes!"

"Would you have gone on without us?" asked Nellie.

"Not a step!" answered Tom, and spoke the words so quickly and earnestly that everybody in the party laughed.

"I didn't want to miss this train for two reasons," went on Dick. "In the first place, we'd lose our parlor-car seats, and in the second place, we'd have to wait four hours for another train, and that nothing but a slow accommodation."

"Well, I shouldn't mind a slow train—while we have such good company," observed Sam, and for this remark Grace gave him a warm look of appreciation.

"Have you had any further news from home?" asked Dick, of Dora, a little later.

"I got a letter from mamma yesterday. She says Professor Crabtree called again. But she had the maid go to the door, and she refused to see him."

"That's good. Did he say anything to the maid?"

"She says he went away looking very angry and muttering something about making mamma see him. Mamma watched him from an upper window and she wrote that he hung around the garden about half an hour before he went away."

"The rascal! You had better get Mr. Laning to look into this for you. If he bothers you any more he ought to be locked up."

"Just what I think. But mamma is too timid to go to the police, or anything like that."

"I wish I was there when old Crabtree called—I'd give him a piece of my mind!"

"Oh, Dick, maybe he would want to—to—shoot you, or something!"

"No, Josiah Crabtree isn't that kind. He belongs to the snake-in-the-grass variety of rascals. But perhaps he won't come again—now that your mother has refused to see him."

"I wish I could be sure of it," sighed the girl.

"What have you done about the fortune, Dora?"

"Mamma has everything in the vault of a safe deposit company in Ithaca. We don't know just what to do—thinking Tad Sobber may tie the money up again in the courts."

"I don't see how he can do that—unless he brings up some new evidence to prove that the fortune belongs to Sid Merrick's estate."

"Uncle John thought it might be best to buy Tad Sobber off—just to end the matter. But Sobber wanted too much."

"I'd not give him a cent—he doesn't deserve it—after the way he treated you, and us. I don't believe Sid Merrick ever had a right to one dollar of the fortune."

"I believe that, too."

"I suppose Crabtree came around because he heard that you had more money than ever. Gracious, Dora, some day you'll be real rich in your own name!"

"Well, won't you like it," she demanded brightly.

"I'll not complain. But I'd take you just as quickly if you were poor," added Dick earnestly.

"Would you, Dick?"

"Do you doubt me?"

"No, Dick, I don't. I know you don't want me for my money," and Dora leaned forward to let her hand rest for a moment on his shoulder.

"I've got a little money of my own," he went on, after a pause, in which they looked straight into each other's eyes.

"A little! Oh, Dick, I guess you've got a good bit more than I've got."

"Are you sorry for that, Dora?"

"Sorry? Oh, no, but—but——" And Dora suddenly turned very red.

"What, dear?" he whispered.

"Why—I—that is—you said you would take me just as quickly if I were poor. Well—I—I'd take you that way, too!" And now the girl hid her blushes in her handkerchief.

"Dora, you're a darling, and true-blue!" whispered Dick, fervidly. "We'll pull together, rich or poor, and be happy, see if we don't!"

"First call for lunch!" announced a waiter, coming through the car.

"Say, that hits me!" came from Tom. "I had such a slim breakfast I am hollow clear to my shoes!"

"A slim breakfast!" sniffed Sam. "Fruit, sawdust and cream, fried eggs with bacon, half a dozen muffins, and coffee!"

"Get out! You're thinking of your own breakfast!" retorted Tom. "Come on, let's lead the way—before the dining car fills up." And he caught Nellie by the arm.

"All right, we're coming!" cried Sam, and followed with Grace. "Come on, Dick!" And he motioned to the others. Soon all were moving towards the dining car.

"Might as well do a little practicing," was Tom's comment, on the way, and linking his arm into that of Nellie, he began very softly to whistle a well-known wedding march.

"Oh, Tom Rover!" cried Nellie, giving him a playful poke in the side. "Of all things! And in a railroad car! I've a good mind not to walk with you."

"All right, I'll change the tune," cried Tom, cheerfully, and commenced to whistle a funeral dirge, at which all of the girls shrieked with laughter.

It was a jolly crowd that sat down to the tables in the dining car, and the Rover boys saw to it that the girls were provided with whatever they desired on the bill of fare. They took their time over the meal, and the fun they had made even the waiters smile broadly.

"We'll get to Cartown in an hour," said Sam, after they had returned to the parlor car. "And then we'll have to say good-bye."

"Oh, it's too bad!" pouted Grace. "I wish you were going through to Cedarville with us."

"So do I."

"Well, the best of friends must part, as the oyster said to the shell," observed Tom, and at this joke the others smiled faintly. But now that they were to separate so soon all felt rather sober. Little did they dream of the exciting occurrence that was to bring them together again.

CHAPTER VIII

HOME ONCE MORE

"And now for Oak Run and home!"

It was Dick who spoke, as he and his brothers boarded another train at Cartown. The girls had gone on in the first train and the boys had had to wait half an hour for the one on the line which would take them close to Valley Brook farm.

"Home it is!" returned Sam. "And I'll be glad to see dad again—and the rest of 'em."

"Right you are, Sam," joined in Tom. "After all, there is no place like home."

"Remember how you used to hate the farm, Tom?"

"Well, that was when we got too much of it. I don't like all farm and nothing else."

"I wonder if Uncle Randolph has any new fads this summer?" came from Dick. Their uncle was more or less of a scientific farmer, and was always trying new ways, and usually losing money on them.

"He's got bees in his bonnet," answered Tom.

"What's that?" demanded Dick, indignantly. "Tom, Uncle Randolph is no more crazy than you are. He has a right to experiment if he wants to."

"Who said he was crazy?"

"You said 'he has bees in his bonnet.' It's the same thing."

"Not much," answered Tom dryly. "He's got bees on the brain—if that suits you better. Aunt Martha wrote me that he had invested in half a dozen hives of bees, and got a queen bee worth I don't know how much to boss the colony."

"Oh, so he's going into bee culture!" murmured Dick. "I hope he doesn't get stung."

"He'll be stung right enough," answered Sam. "If not in one way then in another. He never makes his experiments pay. Say, I rather think I'll steer clear of those bees."

"Maybe we can have some fun with them," mused Tom, and immediately commenced to lay plans for that purpose.

They had a three hours' ride to Oak Run and on the way made several stops of more or less importance. At one place, near the depot, was a cigar store, and Tom left the train and came back with three cigars of large size in his hand.

"What are you going to do with those," questioned Sam, "learn to smoke?"

"No, I am going to treat some of my particular friends," answered Tom, and winked one eye, suggestively.

"Oh, let me in on the joke!" pleaded his younger brother.

"Here it is then," answered Tom, and brought from his pocket a small round wooden box. Taking off the cover he disclosed to view some pellets that were coated with what looked like silver.

"What are they?" questioned Sam.

"The fireworks catalogue called them Serpent's Eggs. You light one and the first thing you know it commences to swell up——"

"Oh, yes, and then pushes out just like a great big worm, or snake!" finished Sam. "I had a box of 'em last year. And are you going——"

"To put them in the cigars. They are harmless, but we can get some fun out of 'em," concluded Tom.

It was an easy matter to cut out a portion of the tobacco from the smoking end of each cigar, and this done Tom inserted three of the pellets in each. Then he placed the cigars carefully in his pocket.

On the way to Oak Run the three lads discussed the doings at Brill, and also the news concerning Tad Sobber and Josiah Crabtree.

"Both of these rascals would like to get their hands on the Stanhope fortune," said Dick.

"Yes, but in different ways," returned Sam.

"Well, neither of 'em shall get his hands on a dollar—if I can help it," answered Dick.

"I should think Crabtree would be ashamed to show himself," went on Sam. "If I was in his place, I'd travel to some new part of the globe, change my name, and make a new try at living."

"In one way I am sorry for him," was Dick's comment. "A man coming out of prison hasn't much chance to get work. Nobody will trust him, no matter if he does want to be honest."

"Do you suppose Crabtree has any money?" asked Tom.

"I don't know, I'm sure."

At last they were only a few miles from Oak Run, and they gathered up the few things they were carrying, fishing rods, cameras, and a small valise.

"Oak Run!" cried the porter.

"Here we are!" exclaimed Tom, the first to get off. "I don't see anything of Jack Ness," he added, mentioning the hired man from the farm, who usually came for them with the team.

"He may be a little late—Jack often is," answered Dick.

"Well, I shan't mind it," said Tom. "I want to see my old friend Mr. Ricks," and he winked at Sam.

The station master at Oak Run was a crabbed old individual who rarely had a pleasant word for anybody. But he was faithful and probably that was why the railroad continued to employ him.

"Why, how do you do, Mr. Ricks, I am real glad to see you!" exclaimed Tom, as he rushed up after the train had gone and caught the station master by the hand. "It seems like old times to get back here."

"Huh! Got back, eh?" muttered Mr. Ricks sourly. "Thought you boys went to college."

"So we did. We are back for the summer holidays. You are looking well, Mr. Ricks."

"I ain't very well, I've got dyspepsy."

"Is that so. Why don't you smoke more?"

"Smoke?"

"Sure. Smoking is the best thing in the world for dyspepsia. Cured the king of England and the emperor of Germany. Here, have a cigar, and see how much better you feel after smoking it."

Now, as it happened, Ricks loved cigars, although he usually smoked a pipe, that being cheaper. He took the big cigar that Tom handed out and started to place it in his pocket.

"Here, light up," cried Tom, and produced a match.

"I'll smoke after I git my ticket money counted up."

"No, light up now," said Tom, and struck the match. "I want you to get the benefit of that cigar at once. It's a special brand and I am sure it will knock that dyspepsia higher than an airship."

Ricks lit up as desired and took several long whiffs from the cigar.

"How do you like it?" questioned Tom, while Sam and Dick watched proceedings closely.

"Putty good," returned the station master. The cigars had cost Tom ten cents each and they were better than those Ricks usually smoked.

A carriage had rolled up to the station and the boys saw Jack Ness coming towards them. He shook hands and then went off to get their trunks and bags, to be placed in a farm wagon driven by a neighbor's boy.

Ricks entered his ticket office and then walked to the back platform of the station, where several farmers were congregated, sitting on some empty milk cans, talking crops. The boys continued to watch him.

"Hullo, where did ye get the smoke?" asked one of the farmers.

"Ricks is gittin' high-toned," said another. "Fust thing you know——"

He got no further, for just then Ricks caught sight of the smoking end of his cigar and his eyes stared wildly.

"What's th—that!" he gasped, and took the cigar from his mouth.

"By gosh! Are ye raisin' snakes, Ricks?" cried one of the farmers.

"Reckon he's struck a nest o' worms!" commented another.

"Wha—what do yo—you think it is?" groaned Ricks. He was so amazed that he could do little but stare at the cigar, from the end of which a snake-like curl was issuing, larger and larger.

"Where did you buy that cigar?" asked one of the farmers.

"Didn't buy it—Tom Rover gave it to me!" answered Ricks. "Say, this is a put-up job!" he roared, and dashed the cigar to the ground. "Where is that imp, anyway?"

"Good-bye, Mr. Ricks!" sang out Tom from the carriage. "Hope you enjoy that smoke."

"You come back here!" stormed the station master. "Just you let me get my fingers on you, that's all!" And he shook his fist at the fun-loving youth.

"It's a trick cigar, that's what it is," announced one of the farmers, and commenced to edge away. "Maybe it will blow up soon."

"If that's so, I'm going to get out!" cried another, and slid from the milk cans in a hurry.

"Say, you don't suppose he put dynnymite in it, do you?" asked Ricks, fearfully. "He might blow up the whole station. He blew up a fire once I was building," he added, referring to a joke Tom had once played on him, the particulars of which have already been set forth in "The Rover Boys at School."

"Better put the cigar in a pail of water," suggested one farmer.

"You do it, Snell."

"Do it yourself, if you want it done," answered Snell, and very gingerly Ricks gathered up the cigar and its "worms" on a shovel and cast them into a tub of rain water that was handy. The others gathered around, joked the station master unmercifully and he vowed that he would get square with Tom sooner or later.

In the meantime the Rover boys lost no time in leaving the railroad station. They had Jack Ness urge on the team, and soon they were crossing the Swift River and driving through the village of Dexter's Corners. Several folks of the village saw them and waved them a welcome, for the lads were great favorites. Then they started along the country road leading to Valley Brook farm.

"And how are all the folks, Jack?" asked Dick.

"All fairly well, sir," answered the hired man. "Your uncle, he got 'em rather bad last week."

"What do you mean?"

"Some of his new bees stung him—and they stung me, too."

"Too bad!" murmured Dick. "Any other news?"

"I don't know of none. The hay crop is going to be heavy, so they say."

"Well, we need hay for the stock."

"We miss you boys, so we do," went on the hired man. "When you are away the farm is like as if we was havin' a funeral."

"Oh, we'll warm you up," cried Tom. "Eh, Sam?"

"We'll try to, anyway," answered the youngest Rover.

"We are going to have a great Fourth of July celebration," said Tom. "I ordered some fireworks for home at the same time I had those sent to the college," he added, to his brothers.

"Yes, we'll have to celebrate in fine style," answered Dick.

They went on, and soon a turn of the road brought them in sight of the farmhouse nestling so cozily among the hills.

"Home again!" sang out Tom. "Let's give them a call!" And he set up a cheer, in which the others readily joined.

"I see dad!" cried Sam, a moment later, as his father appeared around a corner of the house and waved his hand.

"And there is Uncle Randolph, down among his bee hives," added Dick.

"And Aunt Martha is on the piazza!" came from Sam. "And there is Aleck Pop!" he continued, as the ebony face of a smiling negro showed itself from between the trees.

"Boys, I am glad to welcome you home again!" cried Anderson Rover, as the carriage rolled up and the lads leaped out in a bunch.

"And we are glad to see you, dad!" they answered in a chorus, and shook hands. Then Tom made one leap for the piazza and fairly lifted his aunt from her feet. "How are you, Aunt Martha!"

"Oh, Tom, yo—you bear!" gasped Mrs. Rover, but with a beaming face. "My boy, how big you are getting!" And then she kissed him heartily, and kissed the others.

"Back again! and welcome!" said Randolph Rover, as he walked up quickly. Then he, too, shook hands; and all went into the house.

CHAPTER IX

PREPARATIONS FOR THE FOURTH OF JULY

It was a great home-coming. As was to be expected, Aunt Martha had had the cook prepare a most elaborate supper, and, to this the lads did full justice. The long ride on the cars had tired them, yet they remained up long enough to tell about affairs at college, and learn what their father and their other relatives had to say.

"Say, this is like old times!" exclaimed Dick, as he entered his bedroom. "Looks as natural as it ever did."

"Anyt'ing I can do fo' yo' young gen'men?" asked a voice from the doorway, and Aleck Pop showed himself, his mouth on a grin from ear to ear. Indeed Aleck had not stopped grinning since the boys had appeared.

"Not that I know of, Aleck," answered Dick. "How have you been since we went away?"

"I ain't been well, sah," answered the colored man, and his face fell for a moment. "It's been dat awful lonesome lik I thinks I was a gwine to die sometimes."

"Never mind, Aleck, we'll cheer you up some day," came from Tom.

"I guess I ought to be at a boahdin' school, or a collidge," went on Aleck. "Perhaps I'll go back to Putnam Hall—if de cap'n will take me."

"Oh, he'll take you back fast enough," answered Sam. "But why not try for a place at Brill?"

"Yo' collidge? Would da hab me dar, yo' t'ink?"

"Perhaps. They have some colored help."

"Den say, won't you put in a good word fo' me, all ob yo'?" asked Aleck, earnestly. "I'd gib most anyt'ing fo' to be wid yo', 'deed I would!" and his eyes rolled from one lad to another.

"We'll keep that in mind, Aleck," answered Dick. "But you can be with us this summer—at least part of the time."

"I'se glad ob dat, Massa Dick. I'se jess been a-pinin' an' a-pinin' fo' you boys!"

The boys slept soundly, and did not get up until late. They spent the best part of the day in roaming around the farm, and in writing letters to the girls, telling of their safe arrival home.

"I'll tell you what I'd like to do," said Tom, that afternoon. "I'd like to invite the Lanings and the Stanhopes down here to spend the Fourth of July. We might have a sort of house party."

"Great!" shouted Sam. "Just the thing—if they'll come."

"Let us sound dad and Uncle Randolph and Aunt Martha on the subject," added Dick.

The matter was talked over, and the boys readily secured permission to have their friends at the farm for the best part of a week. The invitations were issued immediately, for the national holiday was but ten days off.

"I know what I'd like to do, after they are gone," said Dick. "I'd like to take our tent and go camping up the river for a week or two, just for the novelty of it. We could fish and swim, and take it easy, and have lots of sport."

"Suits me down to the ground," answered Tom. "We'll do it—unless something better turns up."

"I was going to suggest an automobile tour," said Sam. "Uncle Randolph has the new car and it is certainly a dandy."

"Well, maybe we can take the tour, too," answered Dick. "The summer vacation will be pretty long."

"We could run up to Cedarville," said Tom.

"Sure—right to the Lanings' home," added Dick, giving Tom a poke in the ribs.

"Oh, sure—and over to the Stanhopes' place, too."

Having sent their letters the boys waited anxiously for replies. On Saturday the answers came, and they read the communications with deep interest.

"Hurrah! Nellie and Grace are coming, with their mother!" cried Tom.

"And Dora is coming with them," said Dick.

"What about Mrs. Stanhope?" asked Sam.

"She said she might come, but she wasn't sure."

A letter had been written by Mrs. Rover to Mrs. Laning and there was a reply to this, both from Mrs. Laning and Mrs. Stanhope.

"We'll have a great celebration!" cried Tom.

"How about those fireworks?" asked Dick.

"I expect them today."

"Have you got enough?" asked Sam.

"As many as we had at Brill."

"That will be plenty."

"I ordered some powder, too, for use in the old cannon," went on Tom. "We'll wake up the natives this Fourth all right!"

"You look out that you don't blow yourself up," warned Dick, for he knew his fun-loving brother could get rather reckless at times.

"Oh, I'll be on guard," was Tom's answer.

When Tom went to Oak Run to get the fireworks old Ricks was decidedly grouchy.

"I've got a good mind not to let you have 'em," growled the station master. "You didn't have no right to play that trick on me with that cigar."

"What trick?" demanded Tom, innocently.

"Oh, you know well enough, you scamp! Think it's smart to put off a cigar on me thet swells up and busts out worms! Bah! you keep your cigars to yourself after this."

"All right, if you want me to," answered Tom, meekly, and then, watching his chance, he placed another of the "doctored" cigars in Ricks' office, where he had a cigar box with tickets in it. Then he, with Jack Ness' aid, loaded his fireworks and the small box of powder on the farm wagon.

As Tom worked he watched Ricks narrowly and saw the station agent enter his office to sell tickets. While he was making change he chanced to look into the cigar box with the tickets, and Tom, peeping through a crack of the door, saw him take up the cigar and look at it wonderingly.

"Hum!" murmured Ricks. "I thought that box was empty. Sallers must have left this in it when he gave it to me. That's one on Bob. Guess I'll smoke it up before he comes an' asks me about it." The man he mentioned was a storekeeper of the vicinity, who had given him the cigar box the evening before.

Ricks struck a match and commenced to puff away with satisfaction. By this time the wagon was loaded and Tom directed Jack Ness to drive off to the bridge and wait for him.

"Well, good-bye, Mr. Ricks," said the fun-loving youth, as he stepped up to the ticket window. "Hope you don't hold any hard feelings."

"You quit your foolin'!" growled the station master.

"I see you're smoking another cigar."

"What if I am? Ain't I got a right to smoke if I want to?"

"Not if you see things when you do it."

"See things? Wot do you mean, Tom Rover?"

"They tell me that you imagined you saw snakes the other day when you were smoking."

"You go on about your business! You played me a trick, that's what you did!"

"It's queer how cigars affect some people. They get nervous and think the end of the cigar is crawling," went on Tom, earnestly. "Now, if I was affected that way I wouldn't smoke."

"Say, Tom Rover, I want you to understand——"

What the station agent wanted Tom to know was never divulged, for at that instant the cigar commenced to swell at the lit end and then an ashy-colored "worm" commenced slowly to uncurl, reaching a length of a foot or more. Ricks took the cigar in his hand, held it at arm's length and viewed it with horror.

"It's another one of 'em!" he groaned.

"What's the matter, Mr. Ricks?" asked Tom, calmly.

"This cigar! Did—did you play this trick on me?"

"I don't know what you mean."

"Look at the end o' this cigar."

"I don't see anything wrong. It looks like a fine cigar, and it seems to burn well," answered Tom, as soberly as a judge.

"Don't you see the—the worms?"

"Worms! Mr. Ricks you are dreaming!"

"Ain't that a—er—a worm?" shouted the station master, pointing with his finger at the thing dangling at the end of the cigar.

"Mr. Ricks, you must have 'em again," answered Tom, and looked deeply shocked. "You had better go and see a doctor. This cigar smoking has got on your nerves."

"It ain't so! I see the worms! There they are!" And the station master poked his finger into the mass.

Now, as those who are acquainted with the fireworks known as Serpent's Eggs, or Pharaoh's Serpents, know, the "worms" or "serpents" are very fragile and go to dust at the slightest touch. Consequently when Ricks placed his finger rudely on those at the end of the cigar they were knocked off, and falling to the floor, were completely shattered to dust. At this the station master started in amazement.

"Where are the worms?" asked Tom. "I don't see them?"

"Why—I—er—that is—they were here!" stammered Ricks.

"Where?"

"On the end o' the cigar."

"Then where are they now?" demanded Tom. "Give me one, till I examine it."

"Why they—they are—er—gone now."

"Gone?"

"Yes. Say, I don't know about this!" And the old station master commenced to scratch his head. He looked at the cigar wonderingly. But no more "worms" were forthcoming, for the reason that the pellets Tom had placed within had burnt themselves out.

"You certainly ought to see a doctor—or else give up smoking cigars," said Tom, as soberly as ever.

"Tom Rover, ain't this no trick o' yours?"

"Trick? Do you think I am a wizard? I find you smoking a cigar and you go and see worms, or snakes, just as if you had been drinking. Maybe you do drink."

"I don't. I ain't teched a drop in six months."

"Well, you had better do something for yourself," said Tom, as he backed away from the ticket window.

"I don't understand this, nohow!" muttered the old station master. "But I ain't goin' to smoke thet cigar no more!" he added, and threw the weed out on the railroad tracks.

When Tom got to the wagon he was shaking with laughter. The joke was too good to keep, and as they drove along he told Jack Ness about what had occurred.

"It's one on Ricks," said the hired man, with a broad grin. "He's kind o' a superstitious man an' he'll imagine all sorts o' things!"

"Well, if it cures him of smoking it will be a good job done," answered Tom. "I've seen him with a pipe in his mouth when a lady wanted a railroad ticket, and he would blow the smoke right into her face."

It made Randolph Rover somewhat nervous to have so many fireworks and so much powder around the premises—and there was a good reason for this, for the facilities for fighting fire at Valley Brook were very meager. So, to please his uncle, Tom stored the stuff in a small building at the bottom of one of the fields, where some farming implements and berry crates and boxes were kept.

The cannon Tom had mentioned was a rather old affair. But it seemed to be in good condition and the boys spent some time in cleaning it out and putting it in condition for use. It was mounted on a big block and set in the middle of the lawn.

"Now, I reckon we are ready to celebrate!" cried Sam, after all the preparations were complete. "And we ought to have a dandy time."

"We will have," answered Dick.

"Best ever!" chimed in Tom.

CHAPTER X

WHEN THE CANNON WENT OFF

The boys went down to the railroad station in the new touring car to meet Mrs. Laning and the three girls, and possibly Mrs. Stanhope. The car was a fine seven-seat affair, of forty-horse power, and Dick ran it.

"It's the slickest thing in cars I've seen!" cried the eldest Rover boy, enthusiastically. "A tour in it would be great."

"Well, we'll have to take a tour in it before the summer is over," returned Sam.

The train was late and the boys waited impatiently for it to put in an appearance. When it did arrive they were delighted to see that Mrs. Laning had induced Mrs. Stanhope to come along.

"I wanted her to come for two reasons," whispered Dick to Dora, after the first greetings were over. "I wished her here, and I was afraid, if she remained behind, Josiah Crabtree might try to visit her."

"He did try, Dick," answered the girl.

"What, again?"

"Yes, and what do you think? We had another visit from Tad Sobber."

"And what did he say?"

"He wanted us to give him half of the fortune. Said that if we didn't he would never rest until he got the money."

"What did your mother do?"

"She had two hired men, who happened to be at the house, put him out."

"Good! That's the best way to treat him."

"Mamma was very much upset, as you can imagine. And the very next day Josiah Crabtree called, and what do you think he said? He sent word by the maid that he had called not alone on his own behalf, but also on behalf of Sobber."

"Oh, so that's the way the wind blows, eh? They are going to form a sort of partnership, to see if they can't get hold of your money, by one way or another."

"It looks that way, Dick, and I am worried to death."

"I'd like to run Sobber down and put him in prison. He has done a number of things for which he might be arrested."

"I am trying to get mamma to take a trip somewhere. I want her to go in secret, so that Sobber and Mr. Crabtree can't follow her."

"That might be a good thing, Dora," answered Dick, and then he had to turn his attention to running the touring car. Although the automobile was built for but seven, all had crowded in, Sam sitting in front on Tom's lap, and the ladies and girls occupying the tonneau.

The run to the farm took but a few minutes, Dick "letting the machine out" in a manner that made the ladies gasp.

"Never rode so fast in my life, on a country road!" declared Mrs. Laning, on alighting. "It was like a train!"

"Oh, that was nothing," answered Tom. "We can go twice as fast if we want to."

"Not with me in the car!" declared the lady, firmly.

"It's a splendid automobile," said Mrs. Stanhope. "But I shouldn't care to travel at racing speed in one."

The visitors were warmly welcomed by Mrs. Rover and her husband and by the boys' father, and soon all were made to feel at home. The best rooms in the farmhouse were given over to the guests, and Mrs. Rover had placed a beautiful bunch of June roses in each apartment.

"What lovely roses!" cried Mrs. Stanhope. "We have some, but not as grand as these!" And her face showed her satisfaction.

"It's great to have you girls here!" declared Sam. "What a jolly family we would be if we all lived together!"

"Oh, what an idea!" cried Grace, but she smiled even as she spoke.

Of course the boys had to show the girls all over the farm, and Uncle Randolph took the ladies around, showing them the big barns and the cattle, the chickens, the horses, the pigs, and the orchards, and broad fields of corn, wheat, and other products. Then they came back to look at the neat vegetable garden, and Mrs. Rover's flower plots, and also at the bees.

"I hope for great things from my bees," announced Randolph Rover. "I have taken up the study of them with care, and I think I can produce a variety that will give us extra fine clover honey."

"I thought you had your bees all in one place, Uncle Randolph," said Dick, as he noticed a hive set apart from the others.

"That is a new family I bought last week," was the explanation. "I am keeping them apart for the purpose of studying them. But they are rather wild as yet, and I do not dare to disturb them very much."

"Oh, I can't bear bees!" whispered Nellie to Tom. "Let's get out of here," and she walked away, and the others followed.

Although the young folks remained up rather late on the night before the Fourth, Tom, Dick and Sam arranged among themselves to get up early the next day, to fire a salute from the old cannon.

"We'll surprise them all," said Tom. "We'll show 'em we can make a noise even if we are in the country."

The boys crept downstairs at five o'clock and hurried out to the shed where the powder had been left. Bringing the box forth they took it to where the old cannon had been placed on the lawn. The piece was pointed towards an apple orchard, so that it might do no damage.

"Now, fill her up good!" cried Tom. "We want to make as much noise as we can with the first shot."

"Don't put in such a load that she bursts," cautioned Dick.

The powder was measured out and put in, and then this was followed by a wad of paper Sam brought from the kitchen. They rammed the paper in good and tight.

"Now, I guess she's ready to set off," said Tom.

"Tom, don't you stand too close," said Dick. "That cannon might explode. Light the slow match and then run behind a tree, or the corner of the piazza."

"All right, Dick. But I don't think she'll explode," was the reply.

"Hello, goin' to fire her off, eh?" came a voice from the fence, and Jack Ness appeared.

"Yes, Jack," answered Sam. "But keep still—we want to surprise the folks."

"Good enough," murmured the hired man. "You'll do it right enough. Thet old cannon always was a snorter fer noise." And he backed away towards the orchard to get behind a tree, out of the way of possible harm.

All being ready, Tom lit a match and applied it to the slow match of the cannon. Then he ran for the corner of the piazza, to join his brothers.

A few seconds passed—they seemed unusually long just then—but nothing happened.

"The slow match must have gone out," murmured Tom.

"Don't go back!—it may go off, yet," answered Dick. "Sometimes——"

Bang! went the cannon, and the tremendous report echoed and re-echoed throughout the hills surrounding Valley Brook. The charge had been so big that the piece had "kicked back" about a yard.

"Say, that was a noise!"

"If that didn't wake the folks up nothing will!"

"I'm glad she didn't burst."

"So am I."

"By gum, you're celebratin' all right!" came from Jack Ness, as he poked his head from behind a tree. "I guess they must have heard that clear down to the Corners."

"Further than that!" replied Tom.

"Oh, Tom, did you do that?" came a voice from an upper window, and Nellie showed her face.

"What an awful noise!" came from another window, as Dora appeared.

"Did it wake you up?" cried Tom.

"It made me bounce right out of bed!" declared Nellie. "I thought I was shot."

"I thought the house had been hit," said Dora.

"Did your cannon burst?" questioned Grace, as she appeared beside Nellie.

"Not a bit of it!" declared Tom. "Just listen, while we fire another shot."

"Oh, Tom, wait till I put some cotton in my ears!" cried Mrs. Rover, as she showed herself, followed by the others.

"Boys, you didn't shoot off anything in the cannon, did you?" asked Randolph Rover, nervously.

"Nothing but powder and paper, Uncle," answered Sam.

"That ain't so!" suddenly shouted Jack Ness. "By gum! You hit the bee hive, an' here come the bees! Gee, shoo! Git out! Oh, my! I'm stung!" And he started to run from the orchard.

The boys stared for a moment. Down in the orchard was the hive which their uncle had set apart from the others. It seemed to be torn at the top, and a swarm of angry bees were flying around. Part of the swarm had made for Jack Ness, and now the hired man was running for his life.

"Why, I don't see how we hit the hive——" commenced Dick, when a yell from Sam interrupted him.

"The bees! The bees! Some of 'em are heading this way!"

"Hi! hi! don't let 'em fly away!" screamed Randolph Rover. "They are very valuable! Stop them! Make them go back in the hive!"

"Excuse me from touching any bees!" murmured Tom. "I'm going to get out of here!" And he started to run.

"Don't go to the house!" cried Dick. "We don't want the ladies and the girls to get stung. Head for the barn!"

His brothers understood, and they scampered at top speed for the nearest barn. In the meantime they could see poor Jack Ness slashing around wildly with a coat he was carrying.

"Git out o' here, you troublesome critters!" screamed the hired man. "Lemme alone, consarn ye! Oh, my nose! Oh, my eye!" And then he pelted for the vegetable garden. Here he fell over a hot-bed frame and went sprawling. But he soon picked himself up, and then he streaked it down the garden to a patch of corn, gradually outdistancing his little tormentors.

"Say, this is the worst yet!" groaned Tom, and he and his brothers watched the bees from a distance. "However did we happen to hit that hive?"

"I'm sure I don't know," replied Dick, "unless you put something in the cannon. Did you use stones?"

"No. Did you, Sam?"

"Not a thing but that paper. But we rammed that down rather hard."

"I don't think paper would reach to the orchard. Maybe there was something in it. Did you look?"

"No. Come to think of it, it did feel a little hard," answered Sam.

In a few minutes Randolph Rover appeared, followed by the boys' father. The man who was making a study of bees had placed a net over his head and donned gloves, and thus equipped he went down to look at the hive. A small corner of the top had been torn away.

"I fancy the bees will settle down before a great while," said he. "The hive is not much damaged."

"I am glad to hear that, Uncle Randolph," said Tom. "I didn't think that shot would reach so far."

"Next time you had better point the cannon into the air," replied the uncle.

"That's a good idea; we will."

The cook slept at the top of the house, and awakened by the noise came down to the kitchen to start up the fire. She heard the others discussing the discharge of the cannon and mention the damage done to the bee hive. Then she looked around the kitchen and suddenly gave a scream.

"My pocketbook! Where is my pocketbook?"

"Your pocketbook?" asked Sam, who had come around to the kitchen to wash his hands. "Where did you leave it?"

"I had it on that side table. It was wrapped in an old newspaper. I was going to take it up to my room last night and hide it, but I forgot."

"That newspaper!" ejaculated Sam, and turned slightly pale. "If you had it in that newspaper it was your pocketbook that shot the top off that bee hive!"

CHAPTER XI

A DAY TO REMEMBER

"Great Cicero, is it possible we have shot the cook's pocketbook to pieces!" murmured Dick, who had come up in time to hear the conversation.

"Shoot it! Did you shoot at my pocketbook?" demanded Sarah.

"We didn't shoot at it, Sarah," answered Sam. "I stuffed that paper in the cannon for wadding."

"What, with my pocketbook in it!" screamed the cook. "Oh, dear! Was ever there such boys!"

"I didn't know there was anything in the paper. It looked all crumpled up."

"It was the best paper I could find and I thought it would do," groaned Sarah. "Oh, dear, what am I to do? Where is the pocketbook now?"

"Blown to kingdom come, I reckon," murmured the youngest Rover. "But never mind, I'll buy you a new one."

"The pocketbook couldn't have been a very large one," said Tom, who had come up to learn the cause of the excitement in the kitchen.

"It wasn't—it was quite small. My sister sent it to me from Chicago, for a birthday present."

"What did you have in it?" asked Sam anxiously.

"I had four dollars in it in bills, and ten of those new shiny cents, and a ten-cent piece, and a sample of dress goods, and a slip of paper with a new way on it to make grape jelly, and some pills for the headache, and a motto verse, and—and I don't know what else."

"Well, that's enough," came from Tom. "No wonder the bees kicked at having all that fired at 'em."

"I'll give you back the money, Sarah, and get you a new pocketbook," said Sam. "I'm awfully sorry it happened."

"Let's look for the pocketbook," suggested Dick, and this was done, the boys taking good care, while on the search, to keep out of the range of the bees. All they could find in the orchard were two of the cent pieces and part of the metal clasp of the pocketbook—the rest had disappeared.

"Well, let us be thankful that we didn't blow the cannon apart, or hit somebody with that charge," said Dick.

Later the cannon was fired off with more care. It certainly made a loud noise, and a farmer, driving past, said he had heard it away down at Oak Run.

"A feller down there told me he guessed the quarry men were blastin'," he said. "But I said 'twas a cannon. She kin go some, can't she!" And he shook his head grimly as he drove on.

The boys and girls spent the morning in firing off the cannon and in shooting off some firecrackers. Mrs. Rover served an elaborate dinner, and had the dining room trimmed in red, white and blue flowers in honor of the national birthday.

"Do you remember how we spent last Fourth," said Tom, when the meal was about over.

"Indeed I do!" cried Nellie. "Don't you remember that big imitation cannon cracker you set off on the dining room table of the yacht and how it covered all of us with confetti."

"Yes, and how Hans Mueller slid under the table in fright!" added Dick; and then all laughed heartily over an affair that I have already described in detail in "The Rover Boys on Treasure Isle."

"Dear old Hans!" murmured Tom. "I'd like first rate to see him this summer."

"Let us ask him to the farm for a week," suggested Sam.

"All right, we will, along with Fred Garrison," answered Dick.

During the afternoon the boys and girls played croquet and took a short ride in the touring car, and had ice-cream and cake served to them under the trees by Aleck Pop, who wore his waiter outfit for the occasion. Then they sat around until it was dark, and after supper the boys brought forth the fireworks.

"Now, be careful," warned both their father and their uncle.

"We will be!" they cried, and set off the pieces from a field where they could not possibly do harm. The girls and the ladies, as well as the men, watched proceedings with interest.

"Oh, how grand!" cried Dora, as the rockets curved gracefully through the air.

"Beautiful!" murmured Grace.

"I could look at fireworks all night!" declared Nellie.

The fireworks came to an end with a set piece called Uncle Sam. It fizzed and flared brightly, showing the well-known face of the old man and the big hat. Then Tom commenced to pull a wire and Uncle Sam took his hat off and put it on.

"Oh, how cute!" cried Grace.

"Last act!" cried Tom, and set fire to a slow match that was near. Presently some flower pots commenced to send up a golden shower, and then, from a wire between two trees there blazed forth the words "Good Night."

"Well, that was very nice indeed!" was Mrs. Stanhope's comment.

"As nice an exhibition of fireworks as I ever saw," declared Mrs. Laning.

"Just what I say!" cried Mrs. Rover. "The boys certainly know how to get up a show!"

After the fireworks came darkness, but neither the boys nor the girls seemed to mind this. They paired off, and took walks around the house and down the roadway. Perhaps a good many silly things were said, but, if so, there was no harm in them. The only ones who were really serious were Dick and Dora, and seeing this Tom nudged Nellie in the side.

"Looks like they were getting down to business, doesn't it?" he observed, dryly.

"Oh, Tom, hush, they might hear you!" she whispered.

"You'll have Dick for a cousin-in-law some day."

"Well, I shan't mind."

"How about having him for a brother-in-law, Nellie?"

At this suggestion Nellie's face grew crimson.

"Tom Rover, you're the limit!"

"Well, how about it?" he persisted.

"You mean if Sam should marry Grace?" she asked archly.

"Not much—although that may happen too. I mean if you should condescend to marry such a harum-scarum chap like me."

"Oh, Tom!" And now Nellie hid her face.

"Maybe you don't like me, Nellie."

"Why, Tom!"

"You know how much I like you. It's been that way ever since we met on the Cedarville steamer. I know I'm pretty young to talk this way, but——"

"You'll get older, eh?"

"Yes, and I don't want any other fellow to come around—when I'm away."

"How about some other girl coming around when I'm away?"

"There can't be any other girl, Nellie."

"Are you sure?" And now Nellie looked quite in earnest.

"Yes, I'm sure."

"Well then—" her voice sank very low. "There can't be any other fellow! There!"

"Nellie!" he cried. Then he would have caught her in his arms, but she held him back.

"Wait, Tom. I understand, and I am very, very glad," she said, earnestly. "But mamma—she is a little bit old-fashioned, you know. She made both of us—Grace and I—promise not to—to become engaged until we were twenty or twenty-one."

"Oh!"

"So we'll have to wait a little longer."

"I see. But we understand each other, don't we, Nellie?"

"Yes, I'm sure we do."

"And when you are old enough——"

"We'll talk it over again," she answered, and took his arm as if to walk back to the others.

"All right," he said. Then of a sudden he turned and faced her. "And is that all?" he pleaded.

"Oh, Tom, it ought to be!" she murmured.

"But, Nellie!" he pleaded, and drew her a little closer. Then for just an instant her head went down on his shoulder and she allowed him to kiss her. Then they joined the others, both feeling as if they were walking on air.

An hour later found everybody either in the house or on the veranda. Dora sat down to the piano and the other young folks gathered around to sing one favorite song after another, while the old folks listened. They sang some of the Putnam Hall songs, and tried several that were popular at Brill and at Hope.

"I like that even better than the fireworks," murmured Mrs. Stanhope, to Anderson Rover.

"Well, I think I do, myself, Mrs. Stanhope," he answered. And then he drew his rocking-chair a little closer to where the widow was sitting. "It seems to me that Dick and Dora match it off pretty well," he continued, in a lower tone.

"Yes, Mr. Rover. And Dick is a fine young man—your sons are all fine young men. I shall never forget what they have done for me and for Dora."

"Well, they are bright lads, if I do say it myself," answered the father, proudly. "And let me say, too, that I think Dora is a very dear girl. I shall be proud to take her for a daughter."

"No prouder than I shall be to take Dick for a son, Mr. Rover."

"I am glad to hear you say that—glad that the idea is agreeable all around," returned Anderson Rover.

"I shouldn't be surprised if, some day, Nellie and Grace married your other sons."

"Possibly. But they are rather young yet to think of that. Dick is older, even though they go to college together. You see, he got behind a little at Putnam Hall because, when I was sick, he had to attend to a lot of business for me. But he is going ahead fast now. He came out at the head of his class."

"So Dora told me. Oh, he will make his mark in the world, I am sure of it."

"If he does not, it will be his own fault. I shall give him as much of an education as he desires, and when he wishes to go into business, or a profession, I shall furnish him with all the money he may need. I am going to do that for all of the boys—that is, unless the bottom should drop out of everything and I should become poor."

"Oh, Mr. Rover, I trust you do not anticipate anything of that sort!"

"No, at present my investments are safe. But one cannot tell what may happen. Hard times come, banks break, railroads default on their bonds, and a man is knocked out before he knows it. But I don't look for those things to happen."

"Mr. Rover, before I leave I wish to ask your advice about that fortune we brought home from Treasure Isle."

"What about it?"

"Do you think I ought to invest the money, or keep it intact and wait to see what that Tad Sobber does?"

"I should invest it, if I were you. I really can't see how Sobber has any claim."

"Would you be willing to invest it for me? A large part of it really belongs to Dora, you know. I am not much of a business woman, and I would be glad if you would help me in the matter."

"Certainly I will help you to invest, if you wish it," answered Anderson Rover.

"Can I send the money to you?"

"Yes, But wait till I send you word. I want to look over the various offerings in securities first."

At that moment came a call from the parlor. The young folks wanted the old folks to come in and join in the singing, and they complied. As they left the piazza a form that had been hiding behind some bushes nearby slunk away. The form was that of Tad Sobber.

"Thought I'd hear something if I came here," muttered that individual to himself. "Going to turn the fortune over to old Rover to invest, eh? Not much! not if I can get my hands on it!"

And then Tad Sobber disappeared down the road in the darkness.

CHAPTER XII

OFF FOR CAMP

All too quickly for the girls and the boys, the visit of the folks from Cedarville to Valley Brook farm came to an end. During the week the boys took the girls on several trips in the touring car, and once all went for a picnic up the Swift river.

"You must write to us often, Dick," said Dora, on parting. "If you go camping, tell us all the particulars."

"I certainly will, Dora," he answered. "And you let me know all about what you are doing. And don't forget to urge your mother to take a trip somewhere."

The boys had already written to their former school chums and fellow travelers, Fred Garrison and Hans Mueller, and those boys had written back that they would arrive at the farm, with an outfit for camping, on the following Saturday.

"That will just suit!" cried Sam. "We can rest up over Sunday and start for camp Monday morning."

"I'm anxious to see what Hans will bring," came from Tom, who was perusing a long communication from the German American youth. "He seems to have the notion that this outing is to last into cold weather, and that we are going to hunt bears and lions and a few other wild beasts."

"Oh, maybe he is only trying to be funny," answered Sam.

"Hans is funny without trying to be," put in Dick. "Just the same, he is one of the best boys in the world."

Fred Garrison and Hans Mueller had arranged to arrive at Oak Run on the same train, and the Rover boys went to meet them as they had the folks from Cedarville, in the new touring car.

"Here she comes!" cried Sam, as the distant whistle of the locomotive reached their ears. Then the train hove in sight and they saw Fred's head sticking out of one window and Hans' head, out of another.

"Hello, Fred! How are you, Hans!" was the cry.

"Say, is this really the station?" asked Fred, with a grin. "I've been watching milk depots for the last hour."

"This is really and truly the metropolis of Oak Run!" sang out Tom. "Move lively now, or you'll be carried further."

The two young travelers alighted, each with two suit-cases. In addition Fred carried a fishing rod. Hans was loaded down with a fishing rod, a shotgun, a big box camera, and a bundle done up in a steamer robe.

"Hello, Hans, did you just come across the Atlantic?" questioned Dick, as the boys shook hands all around.

"Atlantic?" repeated Hans Mueller. "Not much I didn't, Dick; I come from home, chust so straight like der railroad runs alretty."

"You brought a few things along I see."

"Sure I did. Vy not, of ve go camping by der voods? I got my fishing shtick, and my gun, and a planket, and a camera to took vild animals."

"Going to take their pictures first and then slay 'em, eh?" remarked Tom.

"Dot's it."

"Got your license, I suppose."

"License. Vot license?"

"To snap-shot the lions and tigers and bears, Hans. It costs two dollars and ten cents to snap-shot a bear now, and lions and tigers are a dollar and forty-five."

"Vot?" gasped the German boy. "Do da make you bay to took pictures?"

"Why, didn't you know that? I thought you read the new patent and copyright laws."

"No, I got somet'ing else to do, Dom. By chiminy! Of da charge so much as dot I ton't took no bictures, not much!"

"Well, maybe we can fix it so you won't have to pay any license," returned Tom, calmly. "But jump in—dinner is waiting for us at home."

"Say, what a dandy car!" cried Fred. "I've been anxious to see it ever since you wrote about it."

"Tell us all about dear old Putnam Hall," said Sam to Hans, when the crowd were on the way to the farm, and the German boy told them all the news. Then Fred told about himself, and how he was thinking of going into business with his uncle.

"Where are you going to camp?" asked Fred, just before the farm was reached.

"We thought of going up the Swift river," said Dick. "But maybe we'll go over to Lake Nasco. There is a fine spot up there for camping, and we can have the use of a small sailboat."

"That would be fine, Dick!"

"We'll talk it over tonight—after you have had supper."

Fred and Hans had been at the farm before and the old folks greeted them warmly. As usual, Mrs. Rover had a substantial meal prepared, and it did her good to see how both Hans and Fred relished the things provided. The German youth especially had a good appetite, and he stowed away so much it looked as if he would burst.

"Say, we'll have to take along lots to eat," whispered Sam to Dick. "If we don't, Hans will clean us out in no time."

"Well, we'll take all we need," answered the big brother.

After supper the five lads talked over the plans for camping out, and it was finally decided that they should journey up the Swift River to Lake Nasco. They were to remain in camp for a week or ten days, and possibly two weeks.

As my old readers know, the Swift River could not be navigated around the Falls—those awful falls where the boys had once had such a harrowing experience. But further up, the watercourse was fairly deep and smooth, and from that point the boys decided to take the small sailboat and either sail or row to the lake, two miles further on.

"We'll drive to the boat landing with the farm wagon," said Dick. "Jack Ness can take us, and bring the wagon back."

On Sunday the entire family went to the village church and the visitors accompanied them. In the afternoon the boys inspected their outfits and took it easy. Fred and Hans sent letters home, stating they had arrived safely, and the Rovers sent letters to Cedarville.

"Hans, while you are in camp, don't forget to take a picture of the Pluibuscus," said Tom. "They don't charge to take those."

"Vot is dot?" asked Hans innocently.

"What, didn't you ever see a Pluibuscus!" demanded Tom, in astonishment. "It's a sort of a Cantonoko, only larger. They live in holes, like bears, only they have four wings, located between the sixth and the seventh legs."

"Mine cracious, Dom, vot you talkin' apout, ennavay?" demanded the German boy. "I ton't know no animals vot got legs and vings alretty. Vos da very pig?"

"No, they are not pigs."

"Vot? I tidn't say pig. I say vos da pig—pig—pig. Ton't you understand?"

"Sure I understand. They are not pigs."

"Dot ain't it at all. I say vos da pig—so pig or so pig?" And the German boy put out his hands, first close together and then wide apart.

"Oh, you mean large?"

"Yah, dot's him."

"Oh, they are about the size of a horse, that is, when they are young. As they grow older they get smaller, so that an old Pluibuscus is about the size of a dog. But it's the horns you have to look out for. They are pointed like daggers and very poisonous."

"Du meine zeit! Den I ton't vont to meet none of dose Pluricustibusters, or vot you call dem," and Hans shook his head, decidedly.

"If you see one I advise you to run," put in Sam, who was enjoying the fun.

"Run? You bet my life I run!" cried Hans.

"The best way to get away is to run into the water," went on Tom. "They hate the water. Just run into the lake and duck down and keep hidden for five or ten minutes and the Pluibuscus will walk away in disgust."

"How vos I going to keep mine head under der vater fife oder den minutes?" questioned Hans, in perplexity.

"Oh, take a deep breath," suggested Fred.

"I can't do him so long as dot."

"Poke a hole in the water to breathe through," suggested Dick.

"Say, I guess you vos making fun!" cried Hans, suspiciously. "Maybe dare ain't no Pluicusisduster at all. Dot's—vot you call him?—Yah! He is a fish story!"

"Tom, you're discovered!" screamed Sam, and then there was a roar of laughter. Hans looked a bit sheepish, but took the fun in good part.

"Put I get square, see of I ton't!" he said, shaking his finger at Tom.

Sunday evening there was a light shower and the boys were much worried, thinking it might keep on raining. But the shower passed by morning and the sun came out bright and clear.

"And now ho! for camp!" cried Sam "Come on, the sooner we start the better."

An early breakfast was procured, and the camping outfit, consisting of the tent, their fishing and hunting outfits, blankets and extra clothing, and a quantity of food, canned and otherwise, was loaded on the big farm wagon.

"All ready?" asked Dick.

"All ready, so far as I can see," answered Sam.

"Vait! vait!" cried Hans, "I got to get mine ear coferings!" And he ran back into the house.

"Ear coverings?" queried Tom.

"Yes," answered Fred, with a smile. "His mother made him a pair of coverings of mosquito netting, so that ants or other insects couldn't crawl into his ears while he was sleeping."

"Not such a bad idea," said Dick. "But he needed them more in the West Indies than he'll need them here."

Soon Hans appeared with his ear coverings, and then the lads said good-bye. The whip cracked, and they were off on their outing. Little did they dream of how the holidays were to come to an abrupt end.

The road along the river was a rather rough one and they had to proceed slowly, for fear of jouncing off part of the load. But the lads were in the best of spirits and as they rode along they sang and cracked jokes to their hearts' content. Tom had the last of his "doctored" cigars with him and he passed this over to Jack Ness, and all had a hearty laugh when the hired man lit up and was treated to a dose of the "worms."

"By gum! I might have remembered about them cigars!" murmured the wagon driver. "I laffed at Ricks an' now you got the same laff on me!"

"Never mind, Jack, you buy something worth smoking, when you go to town," said Tom, and slyly slipped a silver quarter into the hired man's palm.

It was noon-time when they reached the spot where they could get the sailboat. This was hired from a man living in the vicinity, and that individual's wife supplied all hands with dinner, for the boys did not want to touch their stores until necessary. Then the sailboat was loaded and the boys got on board.

"We'll have to row," said Dick. "There isn't breeze enough to do any good."

"Well, rowing suits me," cried Sam, and caught up an oar and Tom did the same.

"I'll spell you after a bit," said Fred. "It is not fair to let you do all the work."

"So will I," added Dick.

"Yah, and me," nodded Hans.

"Good-bye, Jack!" cried all, and waved their hands to the hired man.

"Tell the folks not to worry—that we will be all right," added Dick.

"Have a good time!" answered Jack Ness. Then Sam and Tom started to row, and slowly the boat moved in the direction of Lake Nasco.

CHAPTER XIII

HANS MUELLER'S QUEER CATCH

Lake Nasco was an irregular sheet of water, about three miles long by a quarter of a mile wide. It was not very deep, excepting at one spot near the upper end. In the center were several islands, known locally as the Cat and Kittens.

The spot the Rover boys had in mind for their camp was located near the upper shore, where a series of rocks ran out to the deep water. Here would be a good place for the sailboat, and here the fishing would be good and also the swimming.

The whole crowd took turns at rowing, and when the lake was reached Sam and Hans got out their fishing outfits and started to troll.

"I don't know if I can catch anything, but if I am successful, we can have fried fish for supper," said Sam.

"Yum! yum! that would just suit me!" cried Fred. "Fish just caught are so much better than those from the store."

It was not long before Sam felt a tug on his line. He hauled in quickly and found a fair-sized perch.

"Hurrah! first luck!" he cried, his face beaming with pleasure.

"Huh! dot ain't mooch of a fish!" was Han's comment. "Chust vait till you see vot I cotch!"

They continued to troll, and presently Sam hooked a medium-sized pickerel. The fish was game and he had to play it a little before Dick was able to bring it in with the net.

"Say, I guess we had better all try our luck," said Tom. "This sport suits me down to the ground."

"No, Tom, let us get to camp," replied his elder brother. "Remember, we have got to cut poles for the tent and cut firewood, and do a lot of things before we go to bed. You can fish all you please tomorrow."

The boat moved on and soon Hans got a bite. It was another perch, about the size of the one caught by Sam. Then Sam got another, but of a different stripe.

Suddenly Hans' line tightened and the German youth stood up in his excitement.

"Vait! I got a pite!" he cried. "Say, dot is a pig feller I guess!" he added.

They stopped in their rowing and watched Hans try to land his catch. He tugged on the line, which grew taut and threatened to snap.

"Play him a little, Hans," suggested Dick. And the line was let out cautiously. Then Hans commenced to reel in once more. Slowly but surely his catch came closer.

"What have you got, Hans, a maskalonge!"

"Maybe it's a whale!"

"Or a water snake!"

"Cracious, vos der vater snakes here?" questioned the German boy, turning slightly pale.

"Sure there are," answered Tom, readily. "Some of 'em are fifteen and twenty feet long."

"Dom, you vos choking."

"No, I'm not choking," answered Tom. "My breath is regular."

"You know vot I mean."

"Oh, pull in the catch!" cried Fred, impatiently.

"That's the talk!" added Sam. "Say, Hans, you've got something big that's sure."

Slowly but steadily the German youth reeled in, until his bait was within a few feet of the boat. Then from the water came something long and dark and slimy.

"It's a water snake!" yelled Tom.

"Oh my! safe me, somepody!" screamed Hans, and fell back in fright and came close to falling overboard. "Cut der line! Ton't let him pite me!"

"It's no snake!" said Sam, quickly. "But what is it?"

"I'll soon know," answered Dick, and pulled in on the line a little more. Then the object came alongside the boat and the boys set up a shout.

"A piece of old rope!"

"With a knot for a snake's head!"

"And a rock at the other end. This must have been used by somebody for an anchor."

"That's it!"

"Say, vos you sure dot ain't no vater snake?" asked Hans, timidly. He had crawled to the bow of the boat, as far from the line as possible.

"See for yourself, Hans," answered Dick.

Hans went forward cautiously and his eyes opened in wonder. Then a sickly grin spread over his round face.

"Huh! Dot's a fine fish, ain't he? Say, Sam, vos you goin' to fry him in putter oder in lard alretty?" And at this quaint query all the other boys set up a hearty laugh.

"Guess you'd better give up fishing now," said Dick, after the merriment was over. "We've got enough for supper, and the best thing we can do is to reach the end of the lake and fix up our camp for the night. We want everything in first-class shape, so that if a storm comes our things won't get soaked."

"Oh, don't say storm!" cried Fred. "I don't want to see rain."

"We are bound to get some, Fred, sooner or later."

The fishing outfits were put away, and once more the boat moved over the bosom of the lake. They had passed three other boats and saw one camp on the north shore.

"Hope we find the Point deserted," said Dick.

"So do I," answered Tom. "We want to camp all by ourselves this time."

It was not long before they came in sight of the shore and the rocky Point. Not a soul was in sight. They brought the boat around to a little cove and all leaped ashore. Near at hand was the remains of a campfire, but it looked a week or more old.

"Nobody here," said Dick.

"What an ideal spot for camping!" was Fred's comment, as he gazed around. And he was right. The shore sloped gently down to the water's edge, and was backed up by a patch of woods. Among the trees were some rocks, and between them a spring of clear, cold water. Not far off was the cove, where the sailboat could be tied up.

"Well, what's the first thing to do?" questioned Tom.

"Cut poles for the tent, and also cut some firewood," answered Dick. "Bring out the hatchets, fellows!"

Two hatchets had been brought along, and all hands were soon at work, getting the camp into shape and starting a fire. Dick selected the poles for the tent and cut them down and trimmed them. Fred built the fire, and Sam cleaned the fish. Then everybody took a hand at raising the tent and fastening it down tightly with pegs. A trench was dug at the rear of the canvas covering, so that if it rained the water would run off towards the lake. The tent was a large one, and in the rear they stored their extra clothing and food. Then they cut down boughs for bedding and got out their blankets.

"The water is boiling," announced Fred, who had put a kettle on some sticks over the fire.

"Well, now the tent is fixed, we'll have supper," said Dick, who had been made leader. "I reckon we are all hungry enough."

"I know I am," said Sam.

"I dink I could eat a leetle," said Hans, winking one eye laboriously.

"Want a piece of fried water snake, Hans?" asked Tom, dryly.

"No, Dom, I dake a steak from dot Pluibusterduster," answered the German youth, with a grin.

Sam knew how to fry fish to perfection, and soon an appetizing odor filled the air. Fred made the coffee, and boiled some potatoes. They had brought along some fresh bread and cut slices from one of the loaves. They also had a few cookies, made by Mrs. Rover.

"Say, this is the best fish I ever tasted!" cried Dick, when they were eating.

"So I say!" added Fred. "Sam, if you don't mind, I'll take another piece."

"It's the fresh air that tunes up a fellow's appetite," remarked Tom. "Stay out a month and you'll want to eat like a horse."

"Nothing the matter with my appetite at any time," murmured Sam.

"Oh, Hans, what's the matter?" he demanded, as he saw the German lad throw his head into the air.

"He's choking!" exclaimed Dick, leaping up in alarm.

"It—it vo—vos ch—chust a fi—fish pone!" gasped Hans. "He got in mine neck sideways alretty!"

"Better be careful after this," cautioned Dick. "Here, swallow a piece of dry bread. That will help to carry it down." And it did, and then Hans felt better.

As night came on the boys prepared their beds and then gathered around the campfire and talked, and told stories. All were in the best of humor, and they talked of their old schooldays at Putnam Hall, and of the jokes played on the other boys, and on Josiah Crabtree, and on Peleg Snuggers, the general utility man.

"Those were certainly great days," said Fred, almost sadly. "I wish they could come back."

"Well, we've got to look ahead, not backwards," answered Dick.

"How some of the fellows have changed," went on Fred. "Just think of what a bully Dan Baxter used to be!"

"Yes, and now he is a real good fellow, and doing well as a commercial traveler," said Tom.

"It's too bad that Tad Sobber can't turn over a new leaf."

"Maybe he will, some day," came from Sam.

"I don't believe it is in him," answered Dick. "He is not like Dan Baxter was. Dan got awfully hot-headed at times, but Sobber is a regular knave—one of the oily, sneaking kind."

"Have you seen him since his injunction against the Stanhopes was dismissed in court?"

"No, but I have heard from him, Fred. He is after that fortune, still."

"What can he do?"

"We don't know. But he is bound to make trouble, some way or other. It makes me sick to think of it."

"Then let us talk about something else," said Tom; and then the lads branched off into a discussion of how the days to come were to be spent.

"Any big game left around here?" asked Fred.

"Not that I know of, Fred. And you couldn't shoot it anyway—it is out of season."

"Maybe we can get some rabbits."

"They aren't of much account this time of year—and they are out of season, too. We'll have to depend mostly on fishing."

It was nearly ten o'clock before they turned in. Then Sam was so sleepy he could hardly keep his eyes open.

"Anybody going to stay on guard?" asked Fred.

"I don't believe it is necessary," answered Tom. "Nobody will disturb us up there."

The fire was allowed to die down, so that it might not set fire to any surrounding objects, and one after another the boys turned in. Hans was soon snoring, and presently Fred, Dick and Sam dropped asleep. For some reason Tom could not compose himself, and he turned restlessly from side to side.

"Guess I must have eaten too hearty a supper," he murmured to himself. But at last he dozed off, to dream of college and a rousing game on the baseball field.

Dick slept for about an hour. Then, of a sudden, he awoke with a start. He felt a pain in his ankle.

"Wonder what's the matter?" he murmured and sat up. As he did so a weird groan reached his ears. He listened intently, and soon the groan was repeated.

"Hi! what's that?" he asked aloud. But no answer came to his question. Then came another groan, and now thoroughly alarmed, Dick leaped to his feet in the darkness.

CHAPTER XIV

THE HAPPENINGS OF A NIGHT

"What's the matter?"

It was Sam who asked the question. Dick's question had aroused him.

"That is what I want to know."

"What woke you up?"

"I felt something on my ankle—and then I heard several groans."

"Vos somepody call me?" asked Hans, sleepily. "It can't pe morning yet, it's too dark."

"We didn't call you, Hans."

"Hello, what is it?" And now Fred roused up. "What is going on?"

"We don't know," answered Sam, who had been sleeping behind him. "We are trying to find out."

Dick had gone to a post of the tent. Here a box of matches had been placed in a holder and he took one out, struck it, and held it up.

"Why, Tom is gone!" he cried, seeing that the place his brother had occupied was vacant.

"So he is!" murmured Sam. He raised his voice: "Tom! Tom! where are you?"

There was no reply to this call, and all in the tent gazed at each other questioningly. Then the match went out, leaving them in darkness as before.

"I don't like this," muttered Dick, and he made his way outside, followed by the others. Fred had loaded a shotgun and he caught up the piece. Hans walked to the smouldering fire and threw on some dry brushwood which soon caused a glare.

All looked around the tent, but failed to catch sight of Tom. Then they hurried to the edge of the lake, but nobody was there.

"Tom! I say Tom!" yelled Sam. "Where are you?"

All listened, but no reply came back. But they heard a curious noise at a distance up the lake shore.

"Maybe he is in trouble!" cried Dick. "Spread out and look for him!"

One of the boys ran up the shore and one down, and Fred and Hans walked towards the woods, the former carrying the shotgun.

"Do you dink a—a bear cotched him?" asked the German youth, in a tragic whisper.

"I don't know what to think," answered Fred.

Dick had gone up the shore, where the rocks were rather rough. As he came out on the point he heard a peculiar noise and then a yell.

"A home run! A home run!" reached his ears. "Everybody in the game!" And then, to his utter amazement, Tom appeared, running in a queer fashion. He was headed directly for the lake.

"He's asleep! He's got a nightmare!" thought Dick, and as Tom attempted to pass him he caught his brother by the arm.

"Let go—I want to reach home plate!" growled the sleepwalker, and tried to break away.

"Tom! Tom! wake up!" cried Dick, and retaining a firm grip on his brother's arm he shook him vigorously.

"Oh!" groaned Tom at last. "I—what—stop shaking me!" he added, in confusion.

"Wake up, Tom! Wake up!"

"I—er—I am awake! What are you shaking me for?" demanded the fun-loving Rover. He could see no fun in the present proceedings.

"Tom, you've been walking in your sleep," said Dick. He raised his voice. "This way, fellows; I've found him!"

"Where is he?" and Sam came running, followed by Fred and Hans.

"Have I—er—really been walking in my sleep?" asked Tom, sheepishly.

"Doesn't this look like it?"

"Why, where am I?"

"Up the lake shore. We missed you and hurried out to find you. You were just going to run into the lake when I grabbed you."

"Was he really walking in his sleep?" asked Sam.

"Yes, unless he was shamming," answered his elder brother.

"I wasn't shamming," stammered poor Tom. "I—er—I was dreaming about a ball game, and I was—er—trying to make a home run! Say, this is punky, isn't it?" he added, staring at the crowd, blankly.

"It's a good thing Dick came up in time," said Sam. "Supposing you had run into the lake."

"Oh, I guess the bath would have woke him up," said Dick. "But I am mighty glad I stopped him," he added.

"You're not more glad than I am," said Tom. "I guess I ate too much supper. I couldn't sleep at all at first."

"I guess you had better chain yourself fast in the tent after this," remarked Fred. "Dick, it was lucky you woke up."

"Something pressed me on the ankle. It's a little sore yet. I guess Tom stepped on it when he left the tent—but I didn't wake up fast enough to catch him then."

All walked back to the tent and sat down around the campfire to talk the matter over. But nothing new was learned and presently they retired again; and this time all slept soundly until morning.

"First in the lake for a morning plunge!" shouted Sam, as he rushed out. "Come on, everybody, it will wake you up!"

"I'm with you, Sam!" answered Fred, and side by side the pair ran down to the water and plunged in.

"Phew! as cold as Greenland!" spluttered Fred, as he came up.

"It's only the first plunge," answered the youngest Rover. "You'll soon get used to it."

The others followed, Hans being the last to go in. The German youth was on the point of backing out, as the water looked so cold, when Sam came up behind him and sent him in with a rush.

"Wow! wow!" spluttered Hans. "Say, maype dot ain't cold, py chiminy! I vos dink I fell into an ice-house alretty!"

"Swim around and you'll soon get warm," was Dick's advice.

The boys remained in the water less than ten minutes and then lost no time in dressing. Then came a hot breakfast, to which all paid every attention.

It had been decided that they should spend the day in fishing and in resting up, so they took it easy. Some went out in the boat and took a short sail, for a fair breeze was blowing.

"This puts me in mind of the times we used to camp out with the Putnam Hall cadets," remarked Tom. "Only there used to be more of a crowd."

For dinner they had more fish, and also some beans which had been brought along. They also made a pot of chocolate—something that suited Hans especially—and the cookies were not forgotten.

Two days passed, and the boys enjoyed every minute of the time. They took a tramp through the woods back of the camp and found a blackberry patch where the luscious fruit was growing in profusion.

"We'll take all we can carry back to camp with us!" cried Sam, and this was done, and then the youngest Rover took it upon his shoulders to make a huckleberry roly-poly pudding, "just like Aunt Martha's." Perhaps the pudding was not as good as those turned out by Mrs. Rover, but it was good enough, and the boys ate it to the last scrap. Then Fred tried his hand one morning at flapjacks and these they also ate with a relish.

"I dink I makes you some Cherman coffee cake alretty," said Hans, on the day following, and in the afternoon he set to work. Soon he had several kettles, pans and pails filled with flour and water and other things. His hands were full of a pasty mess, and he had some of the stuff on his nose.

"How are you getting on?" asked Dick, when he saw the German youth stop and stare around in perplexity.

"I dink I need anudder dish," said Hans, slowly.

"Great Scott, Hans! You now have about all in the camp."

"Is dot so! Vell, I must but dis stuff someveres, ain't it?" And Hans proceeded to dump the mass in one bowl with that in another. The other lads watched him work with keen interest.

"Want more sugar, Hans?" asked Sam.

"How about salt?" questioned Fred.

"Maybe you want a little more flour?" came from Dick.

"Want to flavor it with peppermint?" asked Tom. "I saw a lot of the stuff growing back of the spring."

"You chust leave me alone!" cried Hans. "Ton't you podder me, oder I makes some mistake."

"I guess he has made several mistakes already," whispered Dick to Fred, as they turned away.

"Shouldn't wonder. But wait and see what he turns out."

They all waited and watched Hans from a distance. The poor German youth worked hard for two hours, baking his stuff over the roaring fire. His face was flushed and he looked far from happy. At last he declared that his coffee cake must be done.

"It certainly looks like coffee," said Tom, as he gazed at the mass, which was shaped like a flower pot and was the color of roasted coffee beans.

"All right, Hans, cut it up and let us try it!" cried Fred, cheerfully.

"Dick, you cut him up," answered Hans, rather faintly.

Dick took the carving knife and set to work. The knife went into the "cake" with ease, but there it stuck.

"What's the matter, Dick?" asked Sam.

"I don't know—the knife is stuck."

"Better let me cut it."

"Go ahead and try your luck, Sam."

The youngest Rover came around and took hold of the knife. He tried to draw the blade free but merely succeeded in raising the "cake" into the air.

"Hello, it sticketh closer than a brother!" exclaimed Tom. "Hans, did you put a porous plaster in that cake?"

"Not much I tidn't!" snapped the German lad. "Here, you gif me dot cake! I cut him ub for you, so quick like neffer vas!"

Very valiantly Hans took the "cake" and the knife and set to work. He had no more success than had Dick and Sam. Finally, in a rage, he lifted knife and "cake" on high and brought them down on a stone with a bang. The "cake" bounced back like a rubber ball and all but struck him in the face.

"Hello, Hans has been manufacturing a football!" cried Tom.

"Vot's der madder mit dot ennahow!" roared the German youth. "I make him chust like mine mudder make him in der old country."

"Hans, did you make the coffee cake with glue?" asked Dick.

"I ton't know how I make him!" groaned poor Hans. "I got me all mixed up, mit eferybody around me! Say, can't you vos got dot knife owid somehow?" he questioned anxiously.

"I'll try a new way," said Dick, and placed the "cake" under his feet. Then he drew on the knife, and it came up between his feet with a sucking sound.

"I guess you can sell that coffee cake for rubber," said Sam.

"Don't you want a slice, Sam?" asked Tom.

"Not today, thank you."

"I dink I drow him into der vater!" cried Hans, and picked up the glue-like mass. Then he ran down to the lake front and balanced it on one of his hands. He gave a throw, but the "cake" did not land in the water as he had intended. Instead it remained stuck to his fingers.

"Can't get rid of it so easily!" cried Dick. "Be careful, Hans, or that cake will be the death of you!"

"Du meine zeit!" groaned the German youth, and then he pulled at the mass until he had it free from his fingers. Then he gave it a kick with his foot, and it went into the lake with a splash.

And that was the first and last time Hans tried to make German coffee cake.

CHAPTER XV

STRANGE NEWS

Several days passed and during that time the lads amused themselves hugely, hunting, fishing, swimming and knocking around generally. Once they had a snake scare. The reptile got in the tent and held possession for nearly an hour, when Dick dislodged it with a stick and Sam ended its life with a stone.

"Say, I ton't like dot!" cried Hans, when the excitement was at an end.

"I don't believe any of us do," answered Dick, dryly.

"I'll be almost afraid to sleep in the tent tonight," added Fred, with a shiver.

"Oh, I guess there was only one snake," said Sam. "But we can look around for more." Which they did, in as thorough a manner as possible. But no more reptiles were brought to light.

On Saturday it rained and the rain kept up all day Sunday. This was not so nice, and the boys remained under shelter most of the time.

"I guess I am a fair-weather camper," observed Fred. "I don't like this a bit."

"Oh, let's have a song!" cried Tom. "And then each fellow can tell a story."

"And then we can play a little music," added Sam. He had brought along a mouth harmonica, and Hans had a jews-harp.

Sunday evening it began to clear, and by midnight the stars were shining brightly.

"The weather will be all right by tomorrow," said Dick, who had been out to look around.

"But the woods will be wet," grumbled Fred.

"Never mind, let us go out in the boat. I'd like to explore the creek running in from the other shore."

"That will suit me, Dick. Maybe we can get an extra lot of nice fish over there."

All of the boys slept soundly and it was nearly eight o'clock when they commenced to get breakfast, and it was almost ten before they were ready to start in the sailboat for the other shore of the lake.

"Hello, here comes a boat!" exclaimed Dick, as he looked down Lake Nasco.

"Two men in it," added Tom. "They seem to be in a hurry, too, by the way the fellow at the oars is rowing."

"Why, it's Jack Ness in the back of the boat!" exclaimed Sam, as the craft drew closer. "That is Pete Hawley rowing."

"Jack must have a message," came from Dick. "Wonder what it can be?"

"Hello, boys!" yelled the Rovers' hired man, as soon as he was within hailing distance. "Got a very particular letter fer you!" And he waved the communication in the air.

"What is it, Jack?" demanded Dick, quickly.

"You jess read the letter, and you'll find out as quick as I kin tell you," answered the man.

"Anybody sick or hurt?" asked Sam.

"Nobuddy hurt—leas'wise not in body, an' nobuddy sick nuther, in the ordinary way. But I reckon your friends from Cedarville is putty sick all the way through, when they think of their loss."

Dick snatched the letter and glanced at it. It was in his father's handwriting and bore only a few lines, as follows:

"Just received a telegram from Mrs. Stanhope, wanting to know if I had received her money, as asked for? Telegraphed back that I had not asked for money and had received none. Then she telegraphed that she had sent money to a certain place at my request. I don't understand this at all. I fear something is wrong, and I am going to Cedarville without delay. Better come home and wait to hear from me."

"Mrs. Stanhope's money?" mused Dick, as he handed the letter to his brothers. "Can she mean the fortune from Treasure Isle?"

"More than likely," answered Tom. "Before we came away father told me she has said something about investing it through him. He was to let her know when he wanted the money."

"But he says in this letter that he didn't send for the money," put in Sam.

"If the money had been obtained under false pretenses I guess it is Sobber's work," murmured Dick.

"More than likely," returned Tom. "Oh, this is the worst yet—and just when we were getting ready to enjoy ourselves, too!"

"Well, we'll have to go back, Tom. Father may need us."

"Sure we'll go back. I couldn't stay here and enjoy myself while I knew that fortune was gone."

"It's too bad on you fellows," said Dick, turning to Fred and Hans. "But you can see how it is."

"Oh, that's all right," answered Fred quickly.

"I dink I got enough of camping owid annaway," came from the German youth. "Maype of we stay here much longer von of dem snakes comes and eats us up alretty, ain't it!"

"The telegrams came yesterday, but I waited until this morning to come here," said Jack Ness. "Your father left for Cedarville on the first train today."

"We'll pack right up and get back," answered Dick.

Although he tried not to show it, he was greatly excited. He was sure that the Stanhope fortune had in some manner fallen into the hands of Tad Sobber, and he wondered if that rascal would be able to get away with it.

"If he does it will be a sad blow to both the Stanhopes and the Lanings," he said to his brothers. "They were planning to get much good out of that money."

"It will be especially hard on the Lanings," said Tom, soberly. "For they are not as wealthy as the Stanhopes."

All of the boys worked with a will, and Jack Ness and the man who had rowed him to camp aided as much as they could. As a consequence in less than an hour the tent was down and packed, and the rest of the camping outfit placed aboard the sailboat. Then the journey for home was begun.

The wind was in their favor, so those in the little sailboat had to do little rowing, and they helped the other boat along. Arriving at the landing on Swift River, they found the farm wagon awaiting them and also a carriage with the best team of horses the Rover farm afforded.

"Thought you young gentlemen would like to go back that way," explained Jack Ness. "I can drive slower with the wagon. I would have brought the auto, only I can't manage that yet."

"I'm glad you thought of the carriage," answered Dick. "Now we can go home in jig time."

The boys entered the carriage, and Dick took the reins and touched up the horses. Away went the spirited team on a gallop, the turnout bouncing from side to side over the rocky road.

"Mine cracious!" gasped Hans, as he tried to hold himself down. "Look owid, Tick, oder we go overpoard alretty yet!"

"Maybe you'd rather ride home with Jack," suggested Tom.

"No, of you can stand him, so can I," answered the German youth, firmly.

Away they went for the Rover farm, up hill and down. Soon they left the river road and then struck a highway where going was much better. Here Dick made the team do their best, and poor Hans was badly scared, thinking the horses were running away.

"Of you can't sthop 'em, ve vos all busted up, so quick like neffer vos!" he bawled.

"They are all right, Hans," answered Sam. "Let Dick alone, he knows how to handle 'em."

"Ain't da running avay?"

"No."

"All right, of you say so," returned Hans, but his face indicated that he thought otherwise.

At last they came in sight of the farm, and drove up to the house by the back way. Their Aunt Martha saw them coming, and ran out to meet them.

"Any more news from the Stanhopes?" asked Dick, quickly.

"Not that I know of," was Mrs. Rover's answer. "Your uncle has gone off to the telegraph office to wait for word from your father."

"I don't think father has reached Cedarville yet," said Sam.

The team was turned over to Aleck Pop and the boys went into the house. There the Rovers read the telegrams which had been received from Mrs. Stanhope. There was also a telegram from John Laning, in which he said he would look into the matter if he could get around, but that he had fallen from the hayloft of his barn and sprained his ankle.

"That will keep him home," said Sam. "Too bad—just when the Stanhopes may need his aid."

"I wish I knew the particulars of the affair—then a fellow would know how to act," said Dick, impatiently.

"Father may send word before night," answered Tom.

"I was sorry to see your father go away," said Mrs. Rover. "He was not very well."

"Not well?" cried Sam. "What was the matter with him?"

"Oh, it wasn't much, but it was enough. You'll remember how he struck his knee on a rock or something, while you were on that treasure hunt."

"Oh, yes, he fell down in the hole," said Tom. "He was so excited at the time he didn't notice the hurt."

"Exactly, Tom. Well, lately that has bothered him quite some, and he had to go to a doctor about it. The doctor told him to be careful of the knee, or it might give him lots of trouble and maybe get stiff."

"Then he shouldn't have gone to Cedarville," said Dick. "We don't want dad to get a stiff leg."

"Say, do you know what?" cried Tom. "I think we ought to got to Cedarville ourselves."

"That's the talk!" cried Sam. "We can't do anything here but suck our thumbs."

"We'll wait until morning and see if any word comes," answered Dick, who did not want to do anything hastily. "Perhaps father may want us to work on the case from this end."

"What about Fred and Hans?" asked Tom.

"They'll go along—part of the way," answered Sam. "They said they would."

"It's too bad to break up their vacation."

"Oh, they understand matters. And, besides, they are both going elsewhere next week," answered Tom.

Impatiently the three Rovers waited for news from their father or from the Stanhopes. At supper time Mr. Randolph Rover returned from Oak Run.

"Here is a telegram from your father, stating he arrived safely at Cedarville," said the boys' uncle. "We ought to get some word late tonight about this mysterious affair."

A little later Tom was outside, walking around the piazza. He was looking on the ground, and presently saw something bright lying at the foot of a bush, and stooped to pick it up. It was a queer-shaped stone, of blue and white.

"I've seen that stone before," he murmured, as he turned it over in his hand. "It doesn't belong to any of our folks. Maybe it is Fred's, or Hans'."

With his find in his hand he entered the house, where the others were just sitting down to the table to eat. He held the stone up to view.

"Any of you lose this?" he asked, and looked at Fred and Hans.

"Dot ain't vos mine," declared Hans, readily. "Vot vos it, a stone from a preastbin?"

"I guess it is from a watch locket," said Tom.

Fred looked at the stone and started.

"Let me see it!" he cried, and held it close to the light. "Well, I declare!" he gasped.

"What about it, Fred?" asked Dick and Sam, in a breath.

"I don't know who this stone belongs to, but I do know that Tad Sobber used to wear one just like it, when he went to Putnam Hall!"

CHAPTER XVI

SOMETHING OF A CLUE

"Tad Sobber!"

The cry came simultaneously from all of the Rover boys.

"Yah, dot's so!" exclaimed Hans. "I remember him now. Vonce I vos ask Sobber vere he got dot sthone."

"If the stone belongs to Sobber—he must have been here!" gasped out Sam.

"Do you think he is around now?" asked Tom, and threw his eyes about the lawn, as if half expecting their enemy to show himself.

"No, he isn't here now—wish he was," answered Dick, bitterly. "More than likely he is miles away by this time—and the Stanhope fortune with him."

"I can't understand this," said Fred. "Unless Sobber has been here, spying on you."

"Maybe he followed the Stanhopes here—to find out, if he could, what had become of the fortune," suggested Sam.

"Sam, I think you've struck it!" almost shouted Dick. "It may be that he came here, heard Mrs. Stanhope ask dad to invest the money for her, and heard dad say that he would let her know when he wanted the cash. Then, perhaps, he went off, and sent Mrs. Stanhope a bogus letter, or telegram, signing dad's name."

"Say, Dick, you're a regular sleuth!" cried Fred. "I guess you've got it straight."

The boys entered the house, and there told their uncle and aunt of what had been found. Randolph Rover looked at the stone with interest.

"It is a curious one," he said slowly. "I do not imagine there are many like it. If this Sobber had one, then this is probably his."

"You didn't see any strangers around the farm, did you?" asked Sam.

"None that I noticed. Of course plenty of folks have passed up and down the main road, and the back road, too."

It was not long after that when Jack Ness drove up with the camping outfit. The boys aided the man in putting the outfit away and also questioned him concerning Sobber.

"There was one man, or young fellow, hanging around," answered Jack Ness. "I tried to reach him, to ask him wot he wanted, but he jumped the orchard fence and got away. I thought he might be a tramp, although he wasn't dressed like one."

"Why didn't you report him?" demanded Dick.

"Oh, everybody was a-havin' seech a good time I didn't want to bother you. I watched the fellow until he was away down the road."

"How was he dressed and how did he look in the face?"

As well as he was able the hired man described the individual he had seen. The clothing counted for nothing, but the face and manner of the person tallied with that of Tad Sobber.

"I guess it was Sobber right enough," was Tom's comment. "We ought to let dad know about this."

"We will let him know—first thing tomorrow morning," answered Dick.

All waited impatiently for some word from Mr. Rover, but none came in until eight o'clock the next morning. Then the telegram was very brief, reading as follows:

"Bad mix-up, money all gone. Better come on and help in investigation."

"Too bad!" groaned Dick. "I am going to start for Cedarville by the first train."

"So am I," added Tom.

"And I," came from Sam.

Then of a sudden all three lads looked at Fred and Hans.

"Don't you mind me at all," cried Fred. "I'll go with you—as far as Marville."

"And I go so far as Ithaca," added Hans. "Py chiminy! I hopes you cotch dot rascal, Tad Sobber alretty quick!"

"So do I hope we catch him," answered Dick.

The Rover boys were so used to traveling that getting ready did not bother them. They knew they could catch a train for Ithaca in two hours and so lost no time in packing their dress-suit cases.

"We'll go to the depot in the auto," said Dick. "Frank Rand can bring the machine back here." And so it was arranged, Rand being an automobile owner living at the Run.

"Oh, boys, I do hope you will take care of yourselves!" cried Aunt Martha, when they were ready to leave.

"Don't worry, Aunty, we'll do that!" cried Sam.

"Here is something to remember me by!" added Tom, and gave her a warm hug and a kiss. Then the others kissed her, and gave a handshake to Uncle Randolph.

Dick brought the automobile out, and in all of the lads piled and Aleck Pop lifted in the dress-suit cases and Hans' bundle. The power was turned on, and off the touring car moved.

"Good-bye!" was the cry from the boys.

"Don't forget to let us know what is happening!" called out Randolph Rover. "And if you need me, don't hesitate to send for me."

Dick turned on more gasolene and advanced the spark, and soon the big touring car was shooting along the country road at a speed of twenty-five miles an hour. They had plenty of time to make the train, but the Rovers were impatient to get to Oak Run, to send a message to their parent, advising him of their coming.

Through the village of Dexter's Corners they dashed, around a corner, and then straight for the bridge spanning Swift River. A farm wagon was making for the bridge from the opposite shore, and there was not room for both vehicles to pass on the bridge.

"Better slow up and wait, Dick!" cautioned Sam, but instead, Dick turned on more power, and away they sailed over the bridge like the wind, and past the farm wagon.

"Phew! that's going some!" cried Fred. "I don't know as I would have nerve to run a car like that!"

"Oh, Dick's a dandy driver," answered Tom, enthusiastically.

Arriving at the station, they went to the telegraph office and asked for messages, and found none. Then word was sent to Anderson Rover at Cedarville. After that the automobile was turned over to Frank Rand, who agreed to take it back to Valley Brook farm that afternoon.

"Off ag'in, eh?" said Ricks, when they bought their tickets. "I don't see why you boys can't settle down fer awhile."

"Smoking any cigars now, Mr. Ricks." asked Tom, dryly.

"If I am, 'tain't none o' your business!" snapped the old station agent.

"I just heard of a new cure for smoker's jim-jams," went on the fun-loving youth. "You take a squash and boil it in lard, and then cut it into thin slices, and——"

"I don't want none o' your cures!" roared Mr. Ricks savagely. "I ain't got no smoker's jim-jams, nor nuthin'. I——"

"But you saw things, Mr. Ricks, you said you did. Worms, and snakes, and strange things——"

"I didn't! I didn't!" howled the old station agent, growing red in the face. "Now you shet up, do you hear? The boys has been pokin' fun enough at me as it is! Everywhere I go they ask me about my smokin'! I'm sick o' hearin' about it, an' I ain't goin' to stand it, I ain't!" And he shook his fist in Tom's face.

"Sorry you feel so bad about it, Mr. Ricks," said Tom coolly. "I only wanted to do you a favor. Now this squash cure is warranted to——"

"Didn't I tell you I don't want to hear about it!" shrilled the station agent. "You mind your business, Tom Rover! I know you! Some day I'll fix you, yes, I will!"

"Oh, Mr. Ricks, I only want to be of service. Now, if you will only listen. This squash cure is warranted——"

"Stuff and nonsense! I won't listen, do you hear? I won't listen!" The station agent was fairly dancing up and down. "I—I—There's the train. Go on with you, and good riddance!"

"Oh, Tom, you'll be the death of Ricks!" laughed Sam, as all of the lads climbed up the steps of the cars.

"Not much! Nothing like that will ever kill him," answered the fun-loving Rover. "He's too tough!"

"He'll get even with you some day," said Dick.

"Let him—I'm willing," answered Tom, calmly. He was so fair-minded that he was willing to take as well as give, when it came to practical jokes.

The train rolled on, and for the time being the boys had little to do but talk over the situation. At a junction point Fred left them. He promised to write and asked them to send him the particulars of what they did.

Just before Ithaca was reached, the train was delayed. As a consequence they missed the last boat for Cedarville that night.

"That's too bad," said Dick. "Now we won't be able to get to the Stanhope place until eleven o'clock tomorrow morning."

"Well, we can send a telegram to dad at Cedarville," said Sam. "And maybe we can telephone," he added.

At Ithaca Hans left them.

"I keeps mine eyes open for dot Dad Sobber," said he. "Of I finds him I let you know."

"That's the talk, Hans!" cried Tom. "You play detective and some day perhaps you'll win a great big leather medal."

"Yah, dot's so," answered the German youth, complacently.

At the telegraph office they sent a message to their father, who had engaged a room at the new Cedarville Hotel. They mentioned that they would go to the Axtell House in Ithaca, and asked him to communicate with them there by telephone.

At the Axtell House a surprise awaited them. Seated in the reading room they found Dan Baxter, the one-time bully of Putnam Hall, but who had reformed and who was now a commercial traveler for a large jewelry concern.

"Why, Dan, you here!" cried Dick, as Baxter, on seeing them, rushed up to shake hands.

"I am," returned the young commercial traveler. "But I didn't think to have the pleasure of seeing you," he added. "Thought you'd be off on a summer vacation somewhere."

"We were off camping, but we came this way on business," answered Sam. "How have you been?"

"First-rate. Don't I look it?" and Dan Baxter smiled openly.

"You certainly do," put in Tom. "Traveling must agree with you."

"It does."

"And business is good?" asked Dick.

"The best ever. And what is more to the point, I've had a raise in salary."

"You mean the one you mentioned when you met us at Ashton," said Tom.

"No, another one. You see, a rival firm made me an offer. My firm heard of it, and they at once came to me, and told me I mustn't think of leaving—and then they tacked another five dollars per week on my salary," and Dan Baxter's eyes beamed.

"Good!" cried Dick. "Stick to it, Dan, and some day you'll be a member of the firm."

"That is what I am working for. Going to stay here over night?"

"Yes."

"Good enough. We can talk things over. I was rather lonely—not having a soul to talk to. And by the way, whom do you think was here some days ago?"

"Tad Sobber?" questioned Dick, quickly.

"Why—er—yes—he was here. But I wasn't thinking of him when I spoke."

"Who were you thinking of?" asked Tom.

"Old Josiah Crabtree. He is out of prison, you know, and he heard I was stopping here, and he came to see me."

CHAPTER XVII

DAN BAXTER'S REVELATION

The announcement that Josiah Crabtree had come to see Dan Baxter filled the Rover boys with interest.

"Did he have much to say?" asked Dick.

"He had a great deal to say," answered Dan. He looked around at several who had entered the reading room "Come up to my room and I'll tell you all about it."

"We will—after we have notified the clerk where we will be," said Dick. "We are waiting for a message from our father."

The boys engaged their rooms and had their dress-suit cases taken up. A few minutes later the whole crowd entered the apartment Dan Baxter occupied. They noticed that it was well-kept and that on the bureau rested a photograph of Dan's father.

"How is he, Dan?" asked Dick, motioning to the picture.

"Fairly well. He is getting old, you know."

"When you see him next, give him our regards."

"I will," answered Dan, and then he motioned the Rovers to seats and sank down on the edge of the bed with something of a sigh. In spite of his success as a commercial traveler Dan could not help but think of his own past and of his father's past. How his father might have prospered, even as the Rovers had prospered, had he followed the path of fairness and honor! He had reformed now, but this reform had come too late in life to enable him to make another start in the business world. Dan was supporting him, and father and son were glad enough to have the Rovers drop their many just causes of complaint against them.

"I can tell you I was much surprised to see Josiah Crabtree," said Dan, after a pause. "I ask him how he happened to be out of prison, and he said he was let go because of his good behavior."

"That would make me laugh," interrupted Tom. "Think of old Crabtree on his good behavior!"

"He said he had been following me up for nearly a week," pursued Dan, and then he paused and his face grew red.

"Following you up?" cried Sam. "What for?"

"Well—er—I might as well make a clean breast of it, fellows—although I hope you will keep it to yourselves. You'll remember how thick Crabtree and I once were?"

"Yes," answered all of the Rovers in a low tone. They could realize how painful the remembrance of it must be to Dan, now.

"Well, he had an idea that I was the same old Dan and ready for new schemes for making money. He had a scheme, and he wanted me to help him work it."

"What was it?" asked Dick.

"Well, you'll remember that he was always crazy after Mrs. Stanhope."

"He was crazy after her money, and Dora's money."

"Exactly. Well, he wanted me to help him in a scheme against Mrs. Stanhope—the same old scheme he tried years ago. He wanted to get her in his power and force her to marry him."

"What! Marry that jailbird!" cried Dick, and his eyes flashed fire. "What a father-in-law Josiah Crabtree would make!"

"That's it, Dick. He talked around the bush a good deal at first, and I led him on, wanting to know what he had up his sleeve. He talked about his affinity and all that, and said that Mrs. Stanhope really wanted to marry him—that she had said so a score of times——"

"The scoundrel! He tried to hypnotize her!"

"I know all that as well as you do, Dick. Well, he said she wanted to marry him, but that her daughter wouldn't let her, being influenced by you and the Lanings. He wanted me to aid him in getting Mrs. Stanhope away from Cedarville, and he said that as soon as they were married he would give me five thousand dollars for helping him to get her."

"Dan!"

"It is true, every word of it. I pumped him all I could, just to get the details of his plot. But he wouldn't give me the details—in fact, I don't think he had the details worked out. When, at last, I flatly refused to assist him he went off the maddest man you ever saw. He warned me not to say a word to anybody, stating that if I did, he would put the police on my track on some old charge. But I made up my mind that I would write to you, and I'd write to Mr. Laning, too—he being Mrs. Stanhope's near relative."

"Where did he go to?" asked Sam.

"I didn't see him the next day, until late in the evening. Then I was over to Grapeton, to see a jeweler there, and when I was coming away an automobile passed me driven by a fellow in a regular chauffeur's costume. On the back seat was Crabtree and a fellow who used to go to Putnam Hall—the fellow who tried to do the Stanhopes out of that fortune in court, Tad Sobber."

"Sobber and Crabtree!" burst out Dick. "They surely must be together in this deal!"

"It certainly looks like it," added Tom.

"I guess Crabtree is bound to have a part of the fortune, even if he can't marry Mrs. Stanhope," said Sam.

"Is Sobber after that fortune again?" questioned the young commercial traveler.

"We are afraid he already has it in his possession," answered Dick. "Now that you have been kind enough to tell your story, Dan, we'll tell ours." And he related the particulars of what had brought them away from the camp at the lake.

"I guess they are both after that fortune," said Dan, after listening to the recital. "It seems to me it all fits in. Sobber wanted to get hold of that cash. He couldn't do it by force, so he had to use cunning. He is not an overly-brilliant fellow, I take it, so he had to get somebody to aid him. In some manner he fell in with Josiah Crabtree. He knew that Crabtree was as smart as he was unprincipled. The two fixed up the plot to get the fortune—and got it."

"I hope they haven't got Mrs. Stanhope, too," murmured Dick.

"I think Crabtree would rather have the money than have the lady," said Dan.

"Well, we'll know all about the case tomorrow," said Sam. "I am dead tired now and am going to bed," he added, looking at his watch.

"What time is it?"

"Quarter to twelve."

"Gracious, Dan, I didn't think we were keeping you up so late!" cried the eldest Rover boy.

"Oh, that's all right, Dick. I'm glad you came—it saved me the trouble of sending that letter."

"You can go to bed," went on Dick, to his brothers. "I'll stay up a bit longer and see if any message comes from dad."

The Rovers left Dan Baxter's apartment, and Sam and Tom retired, both worn out from their day's exertions. Dick went below, to interview the hotel clerk.

"No message yet, sir," said that individual. "If any comes in I will call you."

Dick was about to turn away, when the telephone bell rang. He waited while the clerk listened for a moment.

"Yes, he's here now," he heard the clerk say. "Wait a moment." The clerk turned to Dick. "There's your party now. I'll switch you into the booth yonder."

Trembling with anticipation, Dick hurried to the booth, shut the door and took up the telephone receiver. The wire was buzzing, but presently he made out his father's voice.

"Is that you, Dick?"

"Yes, Dad. Where are you?"

"At the hotel in Cedarville. I just got here a few minutes ago from a run across the lake."

"Across the lake? What for? Did you go after the fortune?"

"No, I went after Mrs. Stanhope."

"Then she is—is gone?" faltered Dick. He could scarcely speak the words.

"Yes. But how did you guess it?" And Anderson Rover's tones showed his surprise.

"Tell me first where she went, and how?" demanded Dick, impatiently.

"We don't know how she went, or just when. It is most mysterious all the way through. Dora is nearly frantic, for she did not know her mother was going. We followed her up and learned that she had crossed the lake in company with some man who wore a heavy, black beard and dark goggles."

"It must have been Josiah Crabtree," cried Dick, and then, in as few words as possible, he told of the meeting with Dan Baxter and what the young commercial traveler had revealed.

"Yes! yes! that must be the truth of it!" said Anderson Rover. "And Crabtree must have been the one who aided in getting the fortune from the bank where it was being kept."

"Never mind the money, dad, just now. Tell me about Mrs. Stanhope."

"I can't tell you any more, Dick. I went across the lake in a launch, but I could get no trace of her on the other side. Now I am going back to the Stanhope house, and send Dora over to the Lanings. I want you to come up here the first thing in the morning," added Mr. Rover.

"I'll be up, and so will Sam and Tom," answered Dick, and then after a few words more the telephone talk came to an end.

Dick slept but little that night. His one thought was of Mrs. Stanhope. What had become of her? Was it possible that Josiah Crabtree had in some way used his sinister influence to get her to leave her home, and would he be able to hypnotize her into marrying him?

"If he does that it will break Dora's heart!" he groaned. "Oh, it's an outrage! We don't want such a scoundrel in the family!" And he grated his teeth in just indignation.

The first boat for Cedarville left directly after the breakfast hour. The Rovers dined with Dan Baxter and then bade the young commercial traveler good-bye.

"I'll keep my eyes open for Crabtree and Sobber," said Dan. "And if I see either of 'em I'll let you know at once."

"Do," said Dick. "Send word instantly—at my expense."

The boys boarded the same little steamer, the Golden Star, which had first taken them up Cayuga Lake, when on their way to become pupils at Putnam Hall. The captain remembered them and spoke to them cordially. But none of the lads was in the humor of talking to outsiders.

As soon as Cedarville was reached they rushed ashore at the well-known dock. They were going to look around for a public carriage to take them to the Stanhope residence, some distance away, when a voice hailed them.

"Why, boys, I am glad to see you!" came in hearty tones, and the next instant they were shaking hands with Captain Putnam, the owner of the school which they had attended so many years.

"We are sorry, Captain, that we can't stop to talk," said Dick, "but we are in a tremendous hurry."

"Yes, and I know why," answered the owner of the school. "I met your father yesterday. Want to go to the Stanhope place?"

"Yes."

"Then come with me. I have my carriage here, and my best team, and I'll take pleasure in driving you there."

"You are very kind," answered Tom. "My! I almost feel as if I was going back to the school!"

"I'd be glad to have you back, Thomas."

"In spite of my pranks, Captain?" and Tom grinned.

"Yes, in spite of your pranks," answered Captain Putnam, promptly.

"And to think we are after Josiah Crabtree!" murmured Sam. "How time changes things!"

"I trust you catch him, and catch that Tad Sobber, too," answered Captain Putnam, gravely.

The team was a spirited one, and the captain knew well how to handle them. Away they flew, through the village and then out on the smooth road leading to the Stanhope place. Dick relapsed into silence. He was thinking of Dora and of the girl's missing mother.

CHAPTER XVIII

A FORTUNE AND A LADY DISAPPEAR

"And that's all I know about it, Dick."

It was Dora who was speaking. She was seated on the sofa with Dick beside her. She had been telling her story and weeping copiously at the same time. He had listened with great interest, and had comforted her all he could. Tom and Sam had gone off with Mr. Rover, to the Laning place, to interview Mr. Laning and his wife and see if they could throw any additional light on the mystery.

What Dora had to tell was not much, and it simply supplemented the story Mr. Rover had already related to his sons.

One day a strange messenger had appeared at the Stanhope house with a letter for Mrs. Stanhope. The communication was very brief and asked the lady to get the fortune from the trust company that was holding it and take it to Ithaca and there meet Mr. Rover. She was to do this in secret, for, as the letter said, Mr. Rover "wanted to make an investment of great importance, but one which must be kept from the general public, or the chance to buy stock at a low price would be lost." The communication had been signed in the name of the Rover boys' father.

Rather ignorant of business affairs, Mrs. Stanhope had taken the first boat she could get for Ithaca and gone to the trust company and gotten from her private box the whole fortune—her own share and also that of the Lanings. There she had gone to the office of the Adrell Lumber Company, where, so the letter stated, Mr. Rover was to meet her.

The Adrell company's office proved to be a small affair on a side street, and on entering Mrs. Stanhope had met the messenger who had delivered the letter to her the day before. He had said that Mr. Rover was expected every minute and had requested her to sit down.

While the lady was waiting, with the fortune in her valise, a telephone had rung and the man in the office had gone to answer the call. He said Mr. Rover wished to speak to her. She had answered the telephone, and someone had spoken to her in a voice she believed to be Anderson Rover's. The party at the other end of the wire had said he was then dickering for some valuable mining shares owned by a rich old man, and said the shares would surely go up to double value inside of a month.

"I can't leave the old man," came over the wire. "Is Mr. Barker there?"

The man in the office had said he was Mr. Barker, and then the man on the wire had vouchsafed the additional information to Mrs. Stanhope that he was an old friend and perfectly trustworthy. Then Mrs. Stanhope had been requested to turn the fortune over to Mr. Barker, who would deliver it to Mr. Rover without delay.

Thinking that all was fair and square, Mrs. Stanhope had delivered the valise to the man, who had gone off with it immediately. He had told her to go home and Mr. Rover would send her word before night about what he had done.

She had returned to Cedarville and to her home and there she had waited patiently to hear from Anderson Rover. No message coming for her, she had at last grown suspicious and sent word to the hotel at which the Rover boys' father was supposed to be stopping. On receiving a reply that he was not there, and had not been there, she grew more alarmed than ever, and then sent the message to Oak Run which so mystified all of the Rovers.

"We have learned that the Adrell Lumber Company went out of business several months ago," explained Dora. "The old signs were left up and the office was rented temporarily to a man who said he wanted to use it for storage purposes."

"And it was rented that way just to fool your mother," returned Dick.

On learning the truth Mrs. Stanhope had been all but overcome. She had sent word to Mr. Laning, but he could not come, having hurt his ankle as already mentioned.

Then, while Dora and her mother were in the house alone, another message had come. It was signed Tad Sobber, and stated that Sobber had the fortune and would return the greater portion of it provided Mrs. Stanhope would allow him to keep ten thousand dollars and promise not to prosecute him. If she agreed to this, she was to meet a certain man in Cedarville, who would take her across the lake, where she could meet Sobber and get back her valise with her precious belongings. She was particularly cautioned to come alone—otherwise the fortune would not be returned.

"And she went across the lake, and that is the last seen or heard of her," said Dora, and then she burst into fresh tears.

"Have you seen anything lately of Josiah Crabtree?" questioned Dick.

"No, but mamma got a long letter from him, in which he said he loved her more than ever and that she had better make up her mind to marry him. The letter was so sickening mamma tore it up and put it in the stove."

"Dora, I hate to alarm you more, but I think Crabtree had something to do with getting your mother to cross the lake."

"What makes you say that, Dick?" she demanded, with a new fear coming into her face.

"I'll tell you," he answered, and then related the particulars of the meeting with Dan Baxter. When he concluded her face was very pale and her hands icy cold.

"Oh, Dick, would that—that monster carry her off and—and force mamma to marry him!" she moaned.

"I can't answer that, Dora. But you'll remember what a strange influence Crabtree used to exercise over her."

"Yes! yes! But mamma was sickly then and her mind was weak. Now she is much stronger."

"I think Crabtree is something of a hypnotist and mesmerist, and there is no telling what such a rascal will do when he sets out for it. He wants that fortune just as much as Sobber wants it. I think they are working this game between them."

"But why would they take mamma away after they had the fortune?"

"Because the fortune is not all in gold. There is some very rare jewelry and precious stones. The thieves would have trouble in disposing of those things unless they had some semblance of a legal right to do so. If Mr. Crabtree was your mother's husband he could take the jewelry and precious stones and sell them, and nobody would prosecute him."

"Oh, Dick, what shall I do?"

"I don't know that you can do anything, Dora. My advice is, that you go over and stay with the Lanings, and let us try to solve this mystery. We'll do all we can, and we'll make the authorities do all they can, too."

"The Cedarville police are of no account—in a matter of such importance."

"I know that. Father sent to New York for a couple of first-class detectives. Perhaps they'll be able to get on the trail quicker than any of us realize." But though Dick spoke thus it was more to allay Dora's anxiety than through any faith in what the sleuths of the law might be able to accomplish.

The matter was talked over a little longer, and then Dora dressed and packed her suit-case and announced herself ready to go to the Laning farm, located some distance away. Dick drove her over. They found the whole household in excitement over what had occurred.

"I declare, that fortune has brought nothing but trouble from the start," said Mrs. Laning, with a deep sigh. "Sometimes I wish we had never heard of it!"

"I shouldn't care so much for the fortune, if only I knew mamma was safe!" answered Dora.

"I am going down to Cedarville and see if I can't get on the trail of the party who took your mother across the lake," said Dick.

"And I'll go along," came from Tom.

"So will I," added Sam.

"I am going to Ithaca, to look into that lumber office business," said Mr. Rover. "I want to get a good description of the fellow who got that valise with the fortune." In his excitement he did not think of his injured knee.

All drove to Cedarville, and there Mr. Rover took the boat down Lake Cayuga. The boys walked along the docks, looking for a man named Belcher, who rented out small boats. They found the fellow at a boathouse, putting a new seat in a rowboat.

"Do you know anything of this affair?" asked Dick, after he had learned how the news of Mrs. Stanhope's disappearance, and the disappearance of the fortune, had spread.

"I was just thinking I might know something," answered Caleb Belcher, slowly. He was known to be a man who never hurried.

"What?" asked the three Rovers, eagerly.

"Well——" The boatman slowly shifted his quid of tobacco from one side of his mouth to the other. "I was thinking I might know a little."

"But what? Tell us, man!" cried Dick. "Don't keep us waiting."

"It ain't much," was the slow reply. "I was out rowing, you understand—coming from the Point to Harden's dock, when I see a boat I didn't know, moving across the lake."

"Yes," said Sam, impatiently.

"She put across the lake, and she had two men and a woman in her. The woman wore a dark dress and a dark veil."

"It must have been Mrs. Stanhope!" cried Dick. "When was this?"

"About the same time they say the lady disappeared."

"Where did the boat go to?" asked Tom.

"Well, I was kind of curious to know whose boat it was, so I watched pretty closely, and she went in over there," and the old boatman pointed with his hand to a spot on the opposite shore where there was a tall rock and a fair-sized cove.

"Take us over there at once and I'll pay you well," said Dick. "Get out two pairs of oars, and we'll help you to row."

Slow though he was, Caleb Belcher was always anxious to earn money, and soon a rowboat was gotten ready and the three Rover boys sprang in. The old boatman followed, and the craft was headed across the lake.

"Who lives near that spot?" questioned Dick, as they swept over the calm bosom of the lake.

"Tony Carew's farm isn't far off," answered the old boatman.

"Anybody else?"

"Not that I know of."

"Do you know this Tony Carew."

"Guess I do—we went to school together, and licked each other more'n a dozen times," and Caleb Belcher chuckled over the recollection.

"All right, show us to his place," said Dick.

As soon as the shore was reached all sprang out of the boat, which was tied to a bush growing nearby. Then Caleb Belcher led the way along a trail that was rather rough. Presently they came to a road and on it an old farmhouse.

"There is Tony Carew now," said Belcher, and pointed to an old man who sat on a bench, smoking.

"I didn't have nuthin' to do with it—you can't mix me up in it!" cried Tony Carew, as soon as Dick stated the object of his visit. "I didn't tech the lady!" And he bobbed his head vigorously. Evidently he was a man easily scared.

"I want to learn if you know anything about it," returned Dick, sternly. "If you do, tell me."

"I didn't tech the lady! I wouldn't tech nobuddy!" howled Tony Carew.

"Did you see her and the men?"

"Yes—but I didn't tech nobuddy, I tell you. I stayed in the barn."

"But you saw her!" cried Dick. "Where did she go? Or where did those men take her?"

"The hull crowd got in a carriage wot was waitin' down the road."

"Whose carriage?"

"I dunno. They had a white hoss an' a black hoss, an' the carriage had the top kinder torn."

"Who was driving?"

"A man with a linen duster, an' a cap pulled away down over his face."

"Which way did they go?"

"That way," answered Tony Carew, and pointed to a side road leading eastward.

CHAPTER XIX

ON THE WAY TO BOSTON

The Rover boys gazed down the road with interest. It ran between a number of tall trees, and looked to be lonely in the extreme.

"Where does it lead to?" asked Sam.

"It's an old road, running to Shaville," answered Tony Carew. "It ain't hardly used any more."

"And that is why those rascals took it," answered Dick. "They wanted to keep in the dark as much as possible. How far to Shaville?"

"'Bout two miles."

"Can you take us over in a carriage? We'll pay you, of course."

"To be sure! But, say, honestly, I didn't have nuthin' to do with carryin' her off!" cried the old farmer.

"I believe you," answered Dick. "But it's a pity you didn't report what you knew to the Cedarville police."

"I didn't want to git in no trouble."

"Want me any more?" asked Caleb Belcher.

"We may want you," answered Dick. "Stay here for a couple of hours, anyway."

"My price is twenty-five cents an hour."

"All right—and there's a dollar on account," and Dick passed the money over.

A fairly good horse and wagon were brought from the barn, and the boys and Tony Carew got in. Then the horse was urged forward, and over the uneven road they bumped, in the direction of the village of Shaville, a sleepy community, with one store, a blacksmith shop, a church, and about a dozen cottages.

When Shaville was reached the boys commenced a diligent search for some news concerning the carriage with the white and the black horse and the dilapidated top. At first they could find nobody who had seen such a turnout, but presently they met a tramp whom Sam stopped, and he gave them news that was surprising.

"I see 'em!" cried the tramp. "Say, boss, give me a dollar an' I'll tell you all I know."

"You'll tell all you know without the dollar!" cried Dick, and grabbed the knight of the road by the collar. "Come now, tell me, quick!"

"Don't hurt me!" yelled the tramp. "I was only foolin'. Course I'll tell you."

He was subjected to close questioning, and from him it was learned that the carriage with the three men and the lady had passed through Shaville and turned towards Latown. The lady had tried to jump from the carriage just while it was passing the tramp, but the men had held her back. He had heard the men mention Latown, and also speak of an automobile.

"One feller was an old gent, who looked like a perfesser," said the tramp.

"That must have been Crabtree," said Tom.

"Can it be that they were going to leave the carriage and take to an auto at Latown?" came from Sam.

"Perhaps," answered Dick. "If they did take to an auto it will be mighty hard to find them."

Tossing the tramp a quarter, they went on their way, and presently reached Latown, and there hurried to the only garage the place possessed. There they learned that the garage owner had rented a touring car out several days before and it had not yet been returned.

"The fellow who rented it was to pay me ten dollars a day, but I didn't think he'd keep it so long," said the man. "He gave me his card."

"Why, it is my card!" ejaculated Dick, on glancing at the pasteboard. "The nerve of him! Of course it was Sobber—or one of his cronies."

It was not until nightfall that the boys learned what had become of the touring car. Then they found a boy who had seen the car, with three men and two women in it, speeding towards the Albany road. This lad took them to the very spot where he had seen the car.

"YOU'LL TELL ALL YOU KNOW WITHOUT THE DOLLAR!"
CRIED DICK.

"One of the ladies was terribly excited," said the lad. "When she saw me, she shouted something and then threw one of her hair combs at me. Here is the comb now."

"It must be Mrs. Stanhope's," was Dick's comment. "She wanted it to be used to trace her by."

"It is hers," said Sam. "I remember, she had a pair of them."

"What did she shout?" asked Dick.

"I couldn't make out, exactly. It sounded like Boston—but I ain't sure."

"Boston?" repeated Dick. "Oh, it can't be! That is too far away."

"They might be headed for Boston. There is a fine road for autos from Albany to the Hub—the old post-road," said Tom.

"I'll telephone along the line and try to find out where they went," answered Dick.

It was not until the next day that word came in from Albany that the automobile had been seen in that city. It had stopped at a garage to have a tire fixed. No one was in it at the time but a young man. He appeared to be in a great hurry, and had paid well for a rapid repair.

From Albany the auto was traced across the Hudson river and to North Adams. But that was the last heard of it.

"I am going to North Adams," said Dick.

"It looks as if they did really go to Boston," said Tom.

"Well, they could make the run in a day if they tried real hard. The distance is only about a hundred and fifty miles."

All of the boys resolved to go to North Adams, and sent word to Cedarville to that effect. In return came a telegram from Mr. Rover, reading as follows:

"Run them down if you possibly can. Do not spare expense."

"As if I would spare any expense!" murmured Dick. "I'd give all I possess to put Mrs. Stanhope back in her home, and put Josiah Crabtree back in prison!"

"And put Sobber in prison, too," added Tom.

In North Adams the lads quite unexpectedly ran into Spud Jackson, who had been spending a few weeks with some relatives in the

Berkshires. Spud was immediately interested in what the Rovers had to tell and proposed something that met with immediate approval.

"My uncle Dan has got a dandy car—fast as they make 'em," said Spud. "Can go about a hundred miles an hour, I guess. Well, he lets me run it whenever I want to. Say the word and we'll start for Boston tomorrow, and make inquiries all along the road."

"Can you have the use of the car, Spud?" asked Sam.

"Positively. Uncle Dan said I could make a tour of the White Mountains if I wished, but I don't care for the scenery much—too much of it, I guess. But going to Boston, to catch those rascals, would hit me plumb."

So it was arranged that they should start eastward in the morning, and in the meantime Dick and his brothers sent out more messages.

"Who do you think the other woman in that touring car can be?" asked Sam.

"I don't know, Sam," answered his eldest brother. "Perhaps some unscrupulous party who was hired by Crabtree to look after Mrs. Stanhope."

"Dad said he had heard that Sobber got his money to go to court from a woman who was his great aunt."

"Well, she may be the one—most likely she is. I am only afraid of one thing."

"What's that?" asked Tom.

"That by some means old Crabtree will force Mrs. Stanhope to marry him before we can rescue her."

"I wonder why she doesn't try to run away," came from Sam.

"Probably she has tried, Sam; but they watch her too closely."

"If they went to Boston, what will they do there?" queried Tom.

"I don't know—maybe take a liner for Europe, or to some other part of the earth. You must remember, they are playing for a big stake."

The touring car that Spud brought around the next morning was certainly an elegant affair. It seated five and was of sixty-horse power. Spud quickly demonstrated that he knew how to run the machine, so Dick did not offer to do so.

"Now you do the bossing," said Spud. "I'll run her anywhere you please, even if you want to go to the top of Mount Washington."

"We are going after that other auto, that's all," answered Dick, grimly.

The weather was ideal for touring and had they not been under such a mental strain the Rover boys would have enjoyed riding greatly. But they could think of nothing but Mrs. Stanhope and the missing fortune.

"I suppose Dora is waiting every hour to hear from us," said Dick.

"Yes, and the Lanings are waiting, too," added Tom.

"And dad, and the folks at home," supplemented Sam.

They had sent a number of messages to Cedarville and now sent another, telling of their plans, and mentioning some towns at which they expected to stop. To this message no answer was returned until they reached Worcester, on the afternoon of the following day.

"Hello, here's news!" cried Dick. "Say, we want to get to Boston just as soon as we can!"

"What is it?" asked the others, quickly.

"Father has received a postal card, mailed from Boston. It is signed by Mrs. Stanhope, and asked for help."

"Does she give any address?" asked Tom.

"He says all there is of the address is 234 Carm. He says the rest is rubbed out."

"Maybe we can find out in a directory what Carm stands for," suggested Spud.

"Exactly, Spud. Say, will you get us to Boston just as soon as possible?"

"I sure will."

"How far is it?"

"About thirty-five miles."

"Then you can make it in an hour."

"Yes, if——" And Spud closed one eye suggestively.

"If what?"

"If they don't arrest us for speeding. It's against the law to run fast, you know."

"Oh, well, we'll have to take a chance," declared Tom. "It's a case of necessity."

As soon as they were outside of the city limits, Spud turned on the gasolene and advanced the spark, until the touring car was making forty and then forty-five miles per hour. On they tore, through Westboro and other places, and then on towards Wellesley.

"Look out, here, that you don't run down any college girls!" warned Dick, as they came in sight of Wellesley College.

"Oh, I wouldn't run down any girls for the world!" answered Spud, as he slowed down a bit. Soon the main street of Wellesley was left behind and on they sped for Newton and the Hub.

"Hi! hi!" came a sudden call from the roadway, and a policeman appeared, waving his hand frantically.

"Sorry, but we can't stop to talk!" flung back Spud, and in a minute the officer of the law became a mere speck in the distance. He had not gotten their number, so could do nothing.

They were just entering Boston proper when a loud report came from one of the rear tires. The car swerved to one side, and Spud had all he could do to keep it from going into a hitching post. Then he shut off the power.

"A blow-out!" announced Tom, as he leaped to the ground.

"That ends running for the present," said Sam.

"So it does," agreed Spud, mournfully.

CHAPTER XX

AN ADVENTURE IN BOSTON

The Rover boys looked at each other inquiringly. They wanted to go on, but did not know what to do about the stalled automobile.

"You go ahead," said Spud, reading their thoughts. "I'll fix the tire, or have it done by some garage man, and I'll see you later."

"Where?" asked Dick.

"I'll go to the Parker House—that is where my uncle always goes," answered Spud.

"Very well—we'll call for you or send a message," said Tom. "Come on, here is a trolley!" And he ran to stop the car. Soon he and his brothers were on board and bound for the heart of the city.

"Say, do you know any street in town that begins with Carm?" questioned Dick, of the car conductor.

"Carm?" repeated the man, slowly. "No, I don't. I don't believe there is such a street."

"Do you know the streets pretty well?"

"I ought to—I drove an express wagon for four years."

"That looks as if we were up against it," said Dick, to his brothers.

"We'll go in a drug store and consult a city directory," answered Sam. "He may think he knows all the streets, but every city has a lot of places even the oldest inhabitant doesn't know."

They rode on a few blocks further and then, seeing a large drug store, alighted from the car and entered the place. A directory was handy, on a stand, and they asked for permission to consult it.

"Nothing like Carm here," said Tom, after they had looked at the alphabetical list of streets. "We are stumped, sure enough."

"Hello! I've got it—I think!" burst out Sam, so loudly that the attention of several persons in the store was attracted to him. "Here is a Varmolet street. Maybe Mrs. Stanhope only heard the name, and thought it was Carmolet. She wrote that down, and the end became rubbed off."

"You may be right, Sam," answered Dick. "Anyway, I guess your idea is worth looking into. I wonder where Varmolet street is?"

They made several inquiries, and at last learned that the street was a narrow and exceedingly crooked affair about half a mile away. They boarded another street car to visit the neighborhood.

"Look who is here!" ejaculated Tom, as he and his brothers sat down.

"Well, I never!" cried Sam.

"Jerry Koswell and Bart Larkspur!" murmured Dick.

It was indeed the two former students of Brill—the lads who had run away after causing the Rovers and some others so much trouble. Both were loudly dressed in summer outing flannels, and each carried an unlighted cigarette in his hand.

"Huh!" grunted Jerry Koswell, as he glared at the Rovers. "Where did you come from?"

"Perhaps we might ask the same question," returned Dick, coldly.

This meeting was not at all to his taste, especially when he and his brothers wished to turn their whole attention to locating Mrs. Stanhope and her enemies.

"Have you been following us?" demanded Bart Larkspur.

"No, Larkspur, we have something of more importance to do," answered Tom.

"Huh! you needn't get gay, Rover!"

"I'll get gay if I wish," retorted Tom, sharply.

"You had better not follow us," came in ugly tones from Jerry Koswell. "If you do you'll get yourselves in hot water."

"See here, Koswell, and you too, Larkspur," said Dick, in a low but distinct tone. "We know all about what you did at Brill—and so do the authorities know it. Just at present we haven't time to bother with you. But some day we may get after you."

"Bah! you can't scare me!" snorted Koswell. Yet his face showed that he was disturbed.

"Are you staying in Boston?" asked Sam, somewhat curiously.

"No, we are bound for a trip up the coast to——"

"Shut up, Jerry, don't tell 'em where we are going," interrupted Larkspur. "It's none of their business."

"Some day we'll get after you," said Dick. "Now we've got to leave you," he added, as the car conductor called out the name of Varmolet street, as Dick had requested him to do.

"You keep your distance!" shouted Koswell after the Rover boys.

"We are not afraid of you!" added Larkspur, and then the car went on again, and the two former students of Brill were lost to view.

"They are off on some kind of a trip," said Sam. "Evidently they have quite some money."

"More money than brains," returned Tom, bluntly. "If their folks don't take 'em in hand, they'll both end up in prison some day."

"Koswell mentioned a trip up the coast," said Dick. "They must be going up to Portland and Casco Bay, or further."

"I'd like to go to Casco Bay myself," said Sam. "It's a beautiful spot, with its islands. Tom Favor was telling me all about it. He spent three summers there."

They had alighted at the corner of Varmolet street and now started to look for No. 234. They had to walk two blocks, past houses that were disreputable in the extreme.

"I don't like the look of this neighborhood," remarked Sam, as they hurried along. "I'd hate to visit it after dark."

"Think of what Mrs. Stanhope must be suffering, if they brought her to such a spot," returned Dick, and could not help shuddering.

Presently they reached No. 234, an old three-storied house, with a dingy front porch, and with solid wooden shutters, the majority of which were tightly closed. Not a soul was in sight around the place.

"Don't ring any bell," warned Sam. "If those rascals are here they may take the alarm and skip out."

"There isn't any bell to ring," answered Tom, grimly. "There was once an old-fashioned knocker, but it has been broken off."

"I think one of us ought to try to get around to the back," said Dick. "If those rascals are here they may try to escape that way."

"That is true," returned Tom. "But let us make sure first that we have the right place. The folks living here may be all-right people, and they'd think it strange to see us spying around."

Dick looked up and down the street and saw a girl eight or nine years old sitting on a porch some distance away, minding a baby.

"Will you tell me who lives in that house?" he asked, of the girl.

"Why, old Mr. Mason lives there," was the answer.

"Mr. Mason?"

"Yes. He's a very old man—'most ninety years old, so they say."

"Does he live there alone?"

"Yes—that is, all the rest of his family are dead. He has a housekeeper, Mrs. Sobber."

"Mrs. Sobber!" exclaimed Dick.

"Yes, sir."

"How old is she?"

"Oh, I don't know—maybe forty or fifty. She's been Mr. Mason's housekeeper for three or four years. If you call on her, you want to look out. She don't buy from agents."

"Why?" asked Dick, innocently. He did not mind that the little girl took him to be an agent.

"Oh, she is too sharp and miserly, I guess. She used to get me to do her errands for her—but she never paid me even a cent for it."

"Anybody else in the house?"

"Not regular. Once in a while a young man comes to see Mrs. Sobber. He ain't her son, but he's some kind of a relation. I think she's his aunt, or great aunt."

"Haven't you seen anybody else coming lately?"

"I've been away lately—down to my grandfather's farm. I came back last night. I wish I was back on the farm," added the little girl, wistfully.

"Never mind, maybe you'll get back some day," said Dick, cheerily. "Here's something for you," and he dropped a silver dime in her lap, something that pleased her greatly.

AN ADVENTURE IN BOSTON

"It's the place!" cried the eldest Rover boy, on rejoining his brothers. "An old man lives here, and a Mrs. Sobber is his housekeeper. She is some relation to Tad, I feel sure. Maybe she is the one who advanced him some money."

"And maybe she is the woman seen in the auto with Mrs. Stanhope," added Tom, quickly.

"I shouldn't be surprised."

"If you are sure of all this, hadn't we better notify the police?" came from Sam. "Remember, we have not only Tad Sobber against us, but also old Crabtree, and one or two unknown men. In a hand-to-hand fight we might get the worst of it."

"That's a good idea, Sam. Run up to the corner and see if you can find a policeman," said Dick.

"I guess I know how to get to the rear of that building," mused Tom. "I'll go through that alleyway and jump the fences," and he pointed to an alleyway several houses away.

"All right, Tom. You do that, and I'll get in the front way somehow. I'm not going to wait another minute. They may have seen us already, and be getting out by some way of which we know nothing."

Thus speaking, Dick mounted the porch and rapped loudly on the door with his bare knuckles. Tom ran off and disappeared down the alleyway he had pointed out.

Dick listened and then rapped again, this time louder than before. Then he heard a movement inside the house, but nobody came to answer his summons. He tried the door, to find it locked.

"Mrs. Sobber, who is that?" asked a trembling and high-pitched voice—the voice of the old man who owned the building.

"Oh, it's only a peddler; don't go to the door," answered a woman.

"I am not a peddler!" cried Dick. "I have business in this house, and I want to come in."

"You go away, or I'll set the dog on you!" cried the woman, and now Dick heard her moving around at the back of the hall.

"Mrs. Sobber, I want you to open this door!" went on Dick, sharply. "If you don't you'll get yourself into serious trouble."

"Want to be bit by the dog?"

"No, I don't want to be bit by a dog," answered Dick. He listened but heard nothing of such an animal. "I don't believe you have a dog. Will you open, or shall I bring a policeman."

"Mercy on us, a policeman!" gasped the woman. "No, no, don't do that!"

"What does this mean?" demanded the old man. "Open that door, Mrs. Sobber, and let me see who is there. I don't understand this. Day before yesterday you brought those strange folks, and now——"

"Hush! hush!" interrupted the woman, in agitated tones. "Not another word, Mr. Mason. You are too old to understand. Leave it all to me. I will soon send that fellow outside about his business."

"This is my house, and I want to know what is going on here!" shrilled the old man, and Dick heard him tottering across the floor. "I'll open the door myself."

"No! no! not yet!" answered the woman.

"Mr. Mason, I want to come in!" cried Dick loudly. "There has been a crime committed. If you don't want to be a party to it, open the door."

"A crime," faltered the old man.

"Yes, a crime. Open the door at once!"

"No, no, you—er—you shall not!" stormed the woman, and Dick heard her shove the old man back.

"Mr. Mason, for the last time, will you let me in?" shouted Dick.

"Yes! yes!" answered the old man. "But Mrs. Sobber won't let me open the door."

"Then I'll open it myself," answered Dick, and hurled his weight against the barrier. It was old and dilapidated and gave way with ease; and a moment later Dick stepped into the hallway of the old house.

CHAPTER XXI

FROM ONE CLUE TO ANOTHER

"Now, what do you want?" asked the old man, as he eyed Dick, curiously.

"I want to talk to that woman, first of all," cried Dick, and he pointed to Mrs. Sobber, who was just disappearing through a door in the rear of the hallway.

"But what does this mean?" went on Mr. Mason, in a faint voice. "I have done nothing wrong." And now he sank on a rush-bottomed chair, all out of breath. He was very old, and his hair and his face were exceedingly white.

"I'll be back and tell you," went on Dick. He could see at a glance that the old owner of the building had had nothing to do with the stealing of the fortune or the abduction of Mrs. Stanhope.

Dick ran to the door at the back of the hallway, to find it locked. He threw his weight against it, but it did not give way.

He was on the point of pushing on the door again, when a cry from the yard reached his ears.

"Dick! Dick! Come and stop them!" It was Tom who was calling.

"I'm coming, Tom!" he yelled back. And then he landed on the door with all his might.

"Don't br—break the door!" gasped the old man. "If you want to get out to the back, go up and down the stairs," and he pointed a trembling finger upward.

Dick understood, and ran up the front stairs three steps at a time. He passed through a short hallway and then reached a stairs, running down to a back entry way. As he went down these stairs there came another cry from Tom.

"Dick! Dick! they are getting away!"

As fast as he could, Dick reached the entryway and threw open the outer door. He came out in a small yard, surrounded on three sides by a high board fence. At the rear was a gate, and this was wide open.

"Tom! you are hurt!" exclaimed Dick, as he caught sight of his brother flat on his back, and with the blood oozing from a cut on his forehead.

"Yes, the rascal hit me in the head with a club!" gasped poor Tom.

"What rascal?"

"Tad Sobber!"

"Where is he now?"

"Ran out of the gate—and a woman just followed him."

"Did you see anybody else?"

"No. Go after 'em," added the injured youth, pluckily.

"Are you badly hurt?"

"I—I guess not. But he gave me an awful crack!" And pulling himself up, Tom staggered to a wood-chopping block and sat down.

Dick waited to hear no more, but made for the gate and ran into an alleyway beyond. This made a turn and came out on a street behind that upon which the house was located. Dick looked up and down the crooked thoroughfare, but could see no signs of Tad Sobber or the woman.

"Did you see a young man and a woman come out of here?" asked Dick, of a boy who was playing with a ball.

"Sure I did," answered the lad.

"Where did they go?"

"Took the auto and went that way."

"An auto?"

"Yes."

"Was it waiting here?"

"Sure."

"Somebody in it?"

"A man was running it. He was here yesterday, too."

"Did you see who he took out yesterday?" went on Dick, growing interested.

"He came twice. Once he had a lady and a gent for passengers. They came out of that alleyway, just as you did."

"When was this?"

"Just about supper time."

Dick ran down the street in the direction the automobile had taken. He could see no signs of the machine, and presently returned to the back yard where he had left Tom. There the pair were joined by Sam.

"We were too late—they got away!" said Dick, with something like a groan in his voice.

"But not too late for Tad Sobber to leave me his card!" muttered Tom, putting his hand to the cut on his forehead.

"We'll have to have that tended to, Tom," said Dick, kindly.

"Oh, it isn't so bad. I'll put some court-plaster on it, after I've washed it."

"I'm sorry, but I couldn't locate a policeman anywhere," said Sam.

"Never mind, I guess a policeman would only be in the way," returned his oldest brother. "He'd ask a lot of questions, and let it go at that. I'm going into the house, and see if I can find out anything."

"Maybe Mrs. Stanhope is in there," cried Sam.

"No—they have taken her off in an auto, I am almost sure of it, Sam."

The three Rover boys entered the old house, to find Mr. Mason walking nervously up and down in the parlor.

"Where is Mrs. Sobber?" he asked anxiously.

"I imagine she has run away," answered Dick. He drew a long breath. "Mr. Mason, I am going to ask you some questions. If you wish to avoid trouble with the authorities, you will answer me directly and truthfully."

"Yes! Yes! I felt that something was wrong!" cried the old man. "I want no trouble, I am too old and respectable. What is it all about?"

"Briefly, a lady has been abducted and a fortune has been stolen."

"Oh, then the lady they said was—er—insane, was not insane at all."

"Did they tell you she was insane?"

"Yes, that is what Mrs. Sobber and one of the men said. They said they were going to take her to a private asylum."

"The villains!" burst out Tom.

"What asylum?"

"I don't know that. But I overheard them talking about taking a boat to Portland."

"Portland?" repeated Dick. "Are you sure they were bound for that city?"

"Oh, I am not sure of anything—I am only telling you what I overheard."

"Please tell us all about those men who came here, and about the lady, and about Mrs. Sobber," pursued Dick.

"Hadn't we better get after the auto?" asked Tom, who believed in action.

"You and Sam can try to hunt it up," answered the elder Rover. "I'll hear all Mr. Mason can tell first. It may give us a direct clue. I'll meet you later at the Parker House."

Sam and Tom went off, and then Dick listened patiently to the rather rambling tale Oliver Mason had to tell. The old man said that he had known Mrs. Sobber when her husband was alive and had hired her to be his housekeeper after the death of his three sisters and his wife.

"She was all alone in the world excepting for a young man named Tad Sobber, who came to see her once in a while," said Oliver Mason. "I didn't like the young man much, but the two had quite some business together."

The old man then told how Mrs. Sobber had gone away for several days, stating she must look after a lady friend who had become insane. She stated that possibly she would bring the lady to the house for a day or two, but that if she did, Mr. Mason need not be afraid, for a doctor and a nurse would come along. Then the lady had arrived, in company with Tad Sobber and two men. He had not been allowed to talk to the woman, the others saying she might become violent in the presence of strangers. Then the lady had been taken away by the men and Tad Sobber the night before, and Tad Sobber had come back for Mrs. Sobber just about the time the Rovers tried to get into the house.

The story was told with such simpleness that Dick felt bound to believe it, and consequently he saw no reason for blaming Oliver Mason, who was, in truth, on the verge of second childhood.

"I must look around and see if those scamps left anything behind," said Dick. "You won't object to that, will you?"

"No! no!" cried the old man. "Only please do not take any of my few belongings."

"I'll not take anything, sir, you can trust me absolutely," answered Dick, readily.

He made a search of the rooms, and especially the apartments occupied by Mrs. Stanhope and her abductors. At first he found little of value, although he picked up a handkerchief that had Mrs. Stanhope's initials embroidered in the corner.

"That is proof positive that she was here," he thought grimly.

In one of the fireplaces he came across some half-burnt letters. He looked them over with care and caught the post-mark, Portland, Me. On one slip he read the following:

easy from Portla
    the schooner *Mary Del*
        as we arrive, I will have
            if not then Slay's Island, where

"Humph! this may prove of value," murmured Dick to himself, and placed the bit of letter in his pocket. Then he hunted around the rooms again, but nothing more came to light.

"Will Mrs. Sobber come back?" asked the old man, when Dick went below.

"I doubt it, sir."

"She must be an awful woman, if what you say is true."

"She is a criminal, Mr. Mason, and so is that Tad Sobber. I would advise you to have nothing more to do with them."

"I must have a housekeeper," whined the old man.

"Then hire somebody you are sure is honest," returned Dick; and a few minutes later he quitted the house.

On his way to the hotel he met Sam and Tom, who had looked in vain for the automobile. In as few words as possible he told his brothers about what Oliver Mason had said, and of the finding of the slip of paper.

"What do you make of it?" asked Sam.

"I think they are going to Portland, either by auto or in a boat," answered Dick.

"That's just what I think," added Tom. "But we may be mistaken."

"Before we go any further, I am going to have that house watched," went on Dick. "I'll hire a first-class detective, and then, if Mrs. Sobber or any of the others come back, we'll have 'em arrested."

They visited a detective agency, and a man was put on the case without delay. Then the Rovers hurried down to the water front, to see if they could get any trace of Mrs. Stanhope there.

An hour's tramping produced no results, and somewhat discouraged, they were on the point of going to the hotel, to meet Spud, when they saw an old sailor come from a restaurant close by.

"My friend," said Dick, addressing the old tar, "I'd like to get some information. Did you ever hear of a schooner in these parts that was called the Mary Del something or other?"

"Mary Del?" repeated the old sailor, twisting his forelock. "Oh, I reckon you mean the Mary Delaway!" he cried. "Sure, I know her. Didn't I see her sail for Portland less than an hour ago!"

CHAPTER XXII

A CHASE UP THE COAST

"You saw her sail for Portland!" cried Sam.

"Less than an hour ago?" exclaimed Tom.

"Where from?" queried Dick, quickly. "Hurry up and tell me—it will be money in your pocket."

"The Mary Delaway sailed from Cruser's dock," answered the old sailor. "That's about four blocks from here. I can show you the place. But you can't get aboard, messmates—she's gone."

"We must catch her!" ejaculated Dick. "No matter at what cost, we must catch her. How can we do it?"

"Can't we follow her in a motor boat, or a steam launch?" asked Tom.

"You can follow her in a tug," said the old tar. "But she is out of sight now."

"Do you know where she is going to land in Portland?" asked Sam.

"No."

"Do you know anybody on board?"

"I know Jack Crumpet. He sailed in the old Resolute with me. I went to see him—that's how I know the Mary Delawaysailed."

"You were on board?" asked Dick.

"No, I wasn't—I saw Jack on the dock. He said as how the cap'n had given orders for nobuddy to come aboard—why, I don't know."

"Well, I know," muttered Dick. "It was to keep their villainous doings secret. Who did you see on the schooner?"

"I saw several men and two ladies. One lady looked kind of excited."

"It must have been Mrs. Stanhope!" murmured Dick. "Come!" he cried. "Let us get some kind of a boat and follow that schooner."

The Rover boys were accustomed to quick action, and they had supplied themselves with plenty of ready cash to use in case of emergency. Consequently, it was an easy matter for them to pick up a steam tug at one of the docks. The captain said he would willingly follow up the Mary Delaway and try to overtake her if he was paid for it.

"Will you go along?" asked Dick, of the old tar. "I want you to aid in picking up that schooner. You know her by sight. I will pay you good wages."

"I've signed articles for a trip to Africy, starting next week Thursday," answered Larry Dixon, for such was the sailor's name.

"We'll get you back long before that time," answered Dick. "And pay you a nice salary in the bargain."

"Then I'm your man, messmate," responded Larry Dixon.

While the steam tug was getting ready to leave, Dick called up Spud on the telephone and acquainted their college chum with what had occurred.

"When will you be back?" asked Spud.

"I don't know," replied Dick. "Better not wait for us. This may prove a long chase."

"Well, I hope you rescue the lady, get back the fortune, and land those rascals in jail," said Spud.

The steam tug carried a crew of six, all good, strong, hearty fellows. In a few brief words Dick and his brothers explained to the captain how matters stood, and Captain Wells promised to aid them all he could in thwarting the plans of the evildoers. He was armed, and said he could lend the Rovers some pistols if they wanted them.

"I reckon the Mary Delaway will take the regular route to Portland—that is, so far as the wind will allow," said the owner of the tug. "We'll follow that route just as fast as our steam will permit. But let me give you a tip. Perhaps it will be better for you to merely follow 'em to Portland, and have them locked up when they reach that place. If you tackle 'em on the high seas they may show fight and get the best of you."

"I'll think that over," answered Dick, slowly. "But meanwhile crowd on all steam and get after them. Never mind using up your coal—we'll pay for it."

The docks were soon left behind, and the black smoke pouring from the funnel told how the fireman was doing his best to make steam. But it was now late, and it would soon become a problem, as to whether it would be advisable to run so fast during the night. They might pass the schooner without knowing it.

"I'll leave the matter to you, Captain Wells," said Dick, after talking the matter over with his brothers. "I'll pay you your regular price for chartering the tug, and one hundred dollars additional if we succeed in rescuing Mrs. Stanhope."

"I'll do my level best for you, Mr. Rover," responded the captain. "I'll talk to my crew." And he did, promising each man an extra five dollars if they succeeded in doing what the Rovers desired. As a consequence every man, including Larry Dixon, was constantly on the lookout for the Mary Delaway.

Inside of an hour Boston Harbor had been left well behind, and then the bow of the steam tug was turned up the coast in the direction of Portland, about a hundred miles distance. The day was now over and the lights on the tug were lit.

"Don't see anything of the Mary Delaway yet," remarked Larry Dixon. "I'm afraid we'll have to shut up shop till mornin'."

"Could the schooner reach Portland by that time?" asked Sam.

"She'd be there early in the morning," answered the old sailor.

"Then we had better run for Portland, too," said Tom. "We might hang around outside the harbor on the watch."

It was a clear night, with no moon, but with countless stars bespangling the heavens. The boys and some of the others remained on the watch, although they could see but little.

"It would be great if we had a searchlight," said Sam.

"Just the thing!" cried Tom. "But we haven't any, so what's the use of talking about it?"

"Might as well try to get some sleep," said Captain Wells, about nine o'clock. "I can call you if anything turns up."

"We'll stay up a couple of hours yet," answered Dick, although the excitement of the day had worn him out.

But not a sight of the schooner was seen, and one after another the Rover boys laid down to get a few hours' sleep. Captain Wells allowed them to rest until six o'clock. By that time they were standing around near the entrance to Portland harbor.

"See anything yet?" asked Dick, as he sprang up from the berth upon which he had been resting.

"Not yet," answered the captain of the tug.

"You don't think they got here ahead of us?"

"No, for we have been here for several hours."

The boys got up and washed, and then had breakfast. In the meantime the steam tug cruised around, and those on board watched eagerly for a sign of the Mary Delaway.

Thus two hours passed. As the time went by the three Rovers grew more anxious than ever.

"What do you make of this, Dick?" asked Tom.

"I don't know what to make of it, Tom."

"It looks to me as if they had given us the slip," said Sam.

"If they didn't come here, where did they go to?"

"I don't know. What did that scrap of paper say?"

"That spoke of Slay's Island. But none of the men on this tug ever heard of such a place."

"That is not to be wondered at, Dick," went on Sam. "I understand there are scores of islands in Casco Bay. It isn't likely these men from Boston would know the names of all of 'em."

They remained around the entrance to Portland harbor until noon and then Dick ordered the captain to run in and land them.

"You might go up and down the docks a bit," he said. "They might have slipped us after all." They entered the harbor, passing the old lighthouse, and soon were within easy reach of the docks. They looked on all sides for the Mary Delaway, but in vain.

"We have missed her!" groaned Dick.

"What are you going to do next?" questioned Tom.

"See if I can't find out in some way where the schooner went to—and also find out where Slay's Island is located."

"We might get a map of Casco Bay. That would have the names of the islands on it," suggested Sam. "I know there are a great many of 'em, some of 'em quite small and others very large."

At last they started to go ashore. They ran up to a dock where the tug was in the habit of landing when at Portland, and the boys walked to the gangplank that was put out for them.

"Look! look!" cried Tom, suddenly, and pointed to a motor boat lying alongside the steam tug.

"Well, I never!" gasped Sam.

The motor boat was a craft of fair size, and very gaudily painted, in red, blue and yellow. It was piled high with suit-cases, bundles and fishing outfits. At the wheel was a tall young man, smoking a cigarette—a stranger to the Rovers. In the bow, also smoking, were two other young men, Jerry Koswell and Bart Larkspur.

CHAPTER XXIII

ABOARD THE MARY DELAWAY

"Hold on there, you!" bawled Jerry Koswell.

"Why, it's the Rovers!" ejaculated Bart Larkspur. "How did they get here?"

"They are following us, that's what!" stormed Koswell. "And I won't have it!"

"What do you want?" asked Dick, as he walked to the end of the tug nearest to the motor boat.

"I want to know what right you've got to follow us?" returned Jerry Koswell, sourly.

"Who said we were following you?"

"Oh, I know you are. Didn't you follow us to Boston, too? I want to know what it means?"

"Maybe it means that we are going to have you arrested," put in Tom, with a side wink at his brothers.

"Arrested!" gasped Larkspur, and turned pale. "You shan't do it!"

"I want you to stop following us," went on Koswell.

"Go ahead—don't talk to them any more!" whispered Larkspur, uneasily. "Let us get away as soon as we can."

"I am not afraid," answered Koswell, boastfully.

"But they may have us locked up!"

"What's the row about?" asked the young man who was at the wheel.

"Oh, it was a row we had at college, Alf. Those fellows were in the wrong, but they made the Head believe otherwise, and we had to—er —resign," answered Jerry Koswell. "Well, go ahead, if you want to," he added.

"Where are you going?" asked Tom, as the motor boat commenced to move from the dock.

"We are bound for——" began the stranger.

"Don't tell them, Alf!" begged Larkspur. "Go ahead—let's get out."

"If you don't tell us where you are going——" began Sam, when Dick stopped him.

"Let them go—we haven't time to bother with them now," said the eldest Rover boy. "We have other fish to fry."

"As you say, Dick. But we ought to scare the wits out of them if nothing else."

"We'll do it—some day," put in Tom.

As the motor boat swept past they saw that the craft was named the Magnet. Soon some other boats coming in hid it from view.

On going ashore, the Rover boys made diligent inquiries concerning the Mary Delaway and at last learned that the schooner was expected by a certain transportation company some time that afternoon, to take on a cargo of lumber for Newark, New Jersey.

"I don't know what we can do excepting to wait," said Dick.

"Let us go down the harbor to meet the schooner," said Tom. "Then Sobber and Crabtree and the others won't have any chance to land in secret."

"Do you think they'll try to land here, Dick?"

"Honestly Tom, I don't. It is more than likely the captain of the schooner will land that crowd on some island before he comes into Portland."

"Slay's Island?"

"Yes—if there really is such a place."

The steam tug left the dock and ran down to the neighborhood of Portland Light. Here they cruised around for nearly two hours, when old Larry Dixon gave a shout:

"I see her! I see her! There's the Mary Delaway!"

"Where?" asked the three Rovers, excitedly.

"There!" And the old sailor pointed with his hand. "I know her by the two patches on her mainsail and the slit in her jib."

The steam tug was headed in the direction of the incoming schooner, and before long the two craft were within hailing distance of each other.

"Aboard the schooner!" cried Dick.

"Aboard the tug!" was the answering hail.

"I want to talk to the captain."

"I'm the captain. What do you want?"

"I want you to lay-to and let me come on board."

"What for?"

"Business."

"I'm in a hurry," snapped the captain of the Mary Delaway, and the Rovers saw that he was a hard looking individual.

"You can suit yourself, Captain. But if you don't let me come on board I'll have you placed under arrest as soon as you reach your dock," said Dick, in the sternest voice he could command.

"Arrest!" roared the master of the schooner. "Don't you talk like that to me, you young whipper-snapper."

"I will talk like that to you—and I'll do just what I said."

"Have me arrested! You must be joking."

"I am not."

"What for?"

"You know well enough."

"Honestly I don't. You have made some mistake."

"Are you going to stop and let me come on board, or not?" went on Dick, as calmly as he could. "If you don't, it's arrest and nothing less. You can take your choice."

"I don't know what you are talking about," growled the captain. "But I suppose I'll have to let you come aboard, to avoid worse trouble."

The schooner was brought around, and not without difficulty Dick leaped aboard, followed by Tom and Sam. The captain of the schooner when he saw that they were only young men, glared savagely at them.

"Now then, explain yourselves!" he snapped, shortly.

"I want to know what you have done with Mrs. Stanhope?" said Dick, thinking it best to come directly to the point.

"Mrs. Stanhope? Who is she?"

"The lady who was abducted by Tad Sobber and Josiah Crabtree and taken on your schooner at Boston."

"Never heard of any of the people you are talking about, young man. You have got hold of the wrong boat."

"No, there is no mistake. You left Boston yesterday afternoon, and you had on board Mrs. Stanhope and her abductors. I guess you are old enough to know what the punishment is for abduction," went on Dick, pointedly.

"Abduction? I ain't abducted nobody, I tell you. You've got hold of the wrong boat. You can search us if you want to."

"Oh, I don't suppose the lady is on board now. I want to know what you did with her."

"Don't know her—never saw her."

"You took her on board, and you were seen doing it," put in Tom.

"Seen!" cried the captain, and gave a start.

"Yes," put in Sam. "Oh, we've got you dead to rights, and the best thing you can do is to tell us at once where she is."

"Say," said the master of the schooner, slowly and thoughtfully. "You tell me the particulars of this matter and maybe I can put you on the track of something. I never heard of any lady being abducted." He saw that he was cornered and that if arrested matters might go very hard with him.

In a few words Dick and his brothers told about how the Stanhope fortune had been stolen and how the lady herself had been abducted and taken to Boston. Then they said they had positive proof that the lady had been taken aboard the Mary Delaway.

"Where is the proof?" asked the captain, and now his voice was not as steady as it had been.

"Well, for one thing, there is a sailor on the tug who saw the lady on your vessel," said Dick. "In the second place I've got a letter, written by one of those rascals, and naming your boat——"

"What! Did any of those lunkheads write it down in a letter?" roared the captain. "If they did——" he stopped, in great confusion.

"Ah, so you admit the crime, do you?" said Dick, quickly.

"No, I don't admit no crime!" growled the captain of the schooner. "I promised to do a little job for two gentleman, that's all—and I did it—and got paid for it."

"What was the job to be?"

"If I tell you, you won't try to drag me into it, will you?" was the anxious question.

"If you don't tell us, you'll surely go to jail."

"I didn't know there was anything wrong, honest I didn't—leastwise at the start, although I had some suspicions later. That feller Sobber and the old gent, Crabtree, along with a Mrs. Sobber, said they had an aunt who was a bit insane, and they wanted to take her to an island up here in Casco Bay, for rest and medical treatment. They hired me to do the job, and paid me well for it."

"And you took them to the island?"

"I did."

"What island?" asked all of the Rover boys.

"A place called Chesoque."

"Chesoque?"

"Yes. The old lobster catchers used to call it Shay's Island, after old Cap'n Shay, of the lobster fleet."

CHAPTER XXIV

OUT ON CASCO BAY

The Rover boys listened with close attention to the statement made by the captain of the schooner and they felt that the fellow was now telling the truth.

"You say you suspected that all wasn't square?" said Dick, after a pause. "What made you do that?"

"Why—er—the way the lady acted. She seemed to be more scared than crazy. But they kept her down in the cabin, so I didn't see much of her."

"When did you land the crowd on the island?"

"About nine o'clock this morning."

"Were you going back there later?"

"No, they said it wouldn't be necessary."

Dick walked to the rail of the schooner and beckoned to the captain of the steam tug.

"This captain says he landed the crowd on Chesoque Island," he called out. "Do you know where that is?"

"I know where she is," put in Larry Dixon, as Captain Wells hesitated in thought. "The lobster catchers used to have a hangout there."

"Where is it?" asked Captain Wells, and the old tar described its location as well as he could.

"Reckon I could pick it up, from what the man says," said the captain of the tug, to Dick.

"All right then," answered the eldest Rover. He turned again to the captain of the schooner. "Now listen to me. I know you and I know your boat. If you have told me the exact truth, well and good. If you haven't—well, you'll have to take the consequences, that's all."

"I didn't abduct nobody. I only did a job and got paid for it," muttered the captain.

"Where are you bound?"

"Portland."

"And after that?"

"Going to—er—take a load of lumber down to Newark, New Jersey."

"Very well—then we'll know where to locate you. Come on!" added Dick to his brothers.

"You can rely on me," said the captain, and spoke quite respectfully. "I'll tell all I know, and so will my men."

"Hello, Jack!" cried Larry Dixon to a sailor on the schooner, and the fellow addressed waved his hand.

"I'll talk to that man a minute," said Dick, to the captain. The latter wished to demur, but Dick gave him no chance. The fellow was told to go aboard the tug, and there Larry Dixon asked him to tell his story. The sailor had little, however, to add to what his captain had said, excepting that the landing at Chesoque Island had been made in something of a hurry.

"Here's a dollar for you," said Dick, on parting. "Whenever the schooner makes a landing anywhere, you send me word where she is," and he gave the tar his home address and also the address of a hotel in Portland.

"Don't try to get me into trouble and I'll tell you everything I know!" shouted the captain of the schooner, as the steam tug went on its way.

"I'll remember you!" answered Dick, somewhat grimly. He did not know whether he could trust the captain or not.

Leaving the entrance to Portland Harbor, the tug steamed up into the waters of Casco Bay, that beautiful spot with its scores of verdant and rocky islands. As it was the height of the summer season they passed many pleasure boats, big and little. Once they passed an island where a big picnic was in progress and they heard the music from a band quite distinctly. They also passed Peak's Island where there was a big, round-topped structure, which the captain of the tug said was a famous summer theater.

"A fellow could certainly have a dandy time here, cruising around among the islands," was Tom's comment.

From Larry Dixon the boys learned that Chesoque Island was away from most of the others, lying far out in the Bay. It was a rocky place, and there was a story that once a band of smugglers had used it for a rendezvous. It was also said to be inhabited by numerous snakes.

"Excuse me, but I don't want to run up against any snakes," said Sam, shuddering.

"Neither do I," added Tom.

"No snakes shall stop me from trying to locate Mrs. Stanhope," said Dick. "More than likely the story about snakes has little foundation to it."

"Like the story about the snakes back of Putnam Hall," said Tom. "Old Farmer Landell said there were thousands of 'em, and he and his son killed exactly five, and only little ones at that."

Presently a distant shore loomed up and after an examination Larry Dixon declared it was the island for which they were seeking.

"Are you sure?" questioned Dick. "This is very important, and we don't want to make any mistake."

"I know the spot," answered the old tar. "See that old building? The lobster catchers used to use that. And see that rock? There is where the old John Spurr struck, in a storm one winter."

"Well, I don't want to strike anything," said Captain Wells, and ordered the engineer to reduce speed. Then, with great caution, they approached what had once been a good dock, but one which was now practically in ruins.

"Hello, there's a motor boat!" cried Sam, as they came closer. Then all looked and saw that a gaudily-painted motor boat was tied up on one side of the old dock.

"Say, that looks like the motor boat Koswell, Larkspur and that stranger had!" ejaculated Dick.

"It is the same!" shouted Tom. "There is the name, Magnet. Now what do you think of that!"

"What do I think?" said Dick. "I think they must be here."

"With Sobber and the others?"

"I don't know about that. I didn't think they knew Sobber."

As the steam tug drew up on the other side of the dilapidated dock, those on board saw three persons rush from the old building nearby. They were Koswell, Larkspur and the fellow who had been running the motor boat.

"Say, I won't have this!" roared Koswell. "You get out of here, and be quick about it!"

"Can't we stop 'em from landing?" asked Larkspur. He was plainly scared.

"You can't land here!" called out the young man who had run the Magnet. "This is private property. I forbid you coming in."

"Private property?" called out Captain Wells.

"That is what I said." And now the young man turned to his companions and a whispered, but animated conversation ensued.

"Who are you?" asked Dick.

"I am Alfred Darkingham. This island belongs to my uncle, John Darkingham. He gave us permission to come camping here, and said we needn't let anybody else come ashore. I forbid your making a landing."

"That's the way to talk, Alf!" cried Koswell, in a low, but earnest voice. "Make 'em stay away."

"Yes! Yes! don't let 'em come ashore!" added Larkspur.

"Mr. Darkingham, I'd like to talk to you," said Dick, as the steam tug bumped against the dock.

"Don't you listen to him, Alf!" cried Koswell. "He only came to make trouble."

"Make him go right away," added Larkspur.

"I want you to leave," ordered Alfred Darkingham. Evidently he was a close crony to the boys who had run away from Brill.

"I want to ask you a few questions," pursued Dick, firmly. "And I'll not go away until you answer them—and maybe not then."

"This is private property, and—"

"You said that before. What I want to know is, Do you know the other persons on this island?"

"There are no other persons."

"I believe otherwise. A lady has been abducted, and I have every reason to believe she was taken to this island."

"Nobody here. I was here yesterday, and all of last week, and I know."

"I think they brought the lady here this morning, about nine o'clock. I'd like to search the island for her."

"It's a trick!" cried Larkspur. "It's a trick to get ashore and play us foul! Don't you let 'em land!"

"There is nobody on this island but ourselves," said Alfred Darkingham. "You can take my word for that."

"Will you let me make a search?"

"I will not. I want you to go away, and at once. This is private property, and if you try to land I'll have the law on you!" And as he spoke the young man looked not only at the Rovers but also at the captain of the steam tug.

CHAPTER XXV

ON CHESOQUE ISLAND

For a moment there was silence. Dick looked at Alfred Darkingham and then at Captain Wells.

"What do you think of this?" he asked of the captain of the tug.

The captain shrugged his shoulders.

"You do as you think best, Mr. Rover," he said slowly. "He can certainly have us arrested if we land without permission. And the authorities have been pretty strict lately—so many folks landing where they hadn't any business to."

"But if Mrs. Stanhope is here?"

"He says there is nobody but his crowd on the island."

"They may be in hiding," suggested Tom.

"If they are, they'll take good care to keep out of your way—if such a thing is possible."

"Let us leave!" put in Sam, in a low voice. "I've got a plan that may bring results."

"What?" demanded Dick.

"I'll tell you as soon as we are out of hearing," returned the youngest Rover.

The steam tug was backed away from the dock. Koswell and Larkspur grinned in triumph.

"Don't you think of coming back!" shouted Koswell.

"If you do, remember we are armed," added Larkspur.

"We'll remember what you have done—don't forget that," answered Dick, with some bitterness. It worried him greatly to have the search for Mrs. Stanhope delayed.

"Now, what is your plan?" asked Tom of Sam, as soon as they were a goodly distance from the island.

"I propose we sail away and pretend to be going back to Portland. Then we can turn and come up on the other side of the island."

"They'll watch for us," said Dick.

"We might land at night."

"Yes, we could do that. But if we wait, we may be losing valuable time."

"I'll run for the next island and sail around that," said Captain Wells. "That may throw them off the scent."

It took the best part of half an hour to gain the next island and round a convenient point. Here the tug was stopped, that they might decide on their next move.

"Oh, come on, let's do something!" cried Tom. "Let us sail for the other side of that island and chance it! If they come after us, we can easily steam away again."

So it was decided, and rounding the island they were at, they set a new course, so that they might reach Chesoque Island at a point directly opposite to where the dock was located. In the middle of the island were several rocky hills, so that the view from one side to the other was completely shut off.

"I'll have to be careful here," said Captain Wells, "I can't afford to strike on the rocks. Those chaps would let us drown before they would come to our assistance."

The steam tug came in slowly. It could not reach the island proper, but stopped at the first of a series of rocks.

"Let me have one of those pistols," said Dick, to the captain, and the weapon was handed over. Then Tom and Sam also armed themselves.

"You had better stand off," went on Dick to Captain Wells. "If we want you we'll fire three shots, or wave a handkerchief."

"Say, don't you want me along?" asked Larry Dixon. "I'd like a scrap, if it comes to that."

"Come along if you want to," answered Dick. He saw that though the sailor was old he was strong, and not afraid to take his own part.

The boys and the tar lost no time in jumping from one rock to another until the main portion of the island was gained. Then they ran for the shelter of some bushes. In the meantime the steam tug moved away to such a distance that those aboard could be seen with difficulty.

"Now, if the others didn't see us land, we are all right," cried Tom.

"We don't want to make any noise," cautioned Dick. "Remember, they may be on the watch for us—Koswell and his cronies, and the Sobber crowd too."

"Do you think Koswell and Larkspur would give aid to those other rascals?" asked Sam.

"I think they'd do almost anything to make trouble for us, Sam. You can see how bitter they acted at the dock."

With caution the party of four began a tour of the island. They moved from the shelter of the bushes to a thicket of pines, and then climbed along a ridge of rough rocks.

"I'll crawl to the top," said Dick. "Then I'll have a pretty good chance to look around."

At the top of the ridge, however, he found the view somewhat disappointing. There were other ridges, and several thickets of pines and hemlocks, and at one point what looked to be a cliff with some caves beneath.

"It will take some time to explore this island," said he, as he came down. "I don't wonder that the smugglers used to use it. It's got a number of dandy hiding places."

"How in the world did the Sobber crowd learn of it?" asked Sam.

"I think I can answer that," said Tom "Josiah Crabtree once taught in a Portland school and he used to put in his summers on an island in this bay. More than likely, in cruising around, he heard of this island, and when he plotted to abduct Mrs. Stanhope he made up his mind it would be just the spot to bring her to."

"All providing she is here," added Sam. "We haven't proved that yet."

They moved on, and passed another ridge of rocks. Then they came to a well-defined trail, running from one end of the island to the other.

"Let us follow this," said Dick. "If there are any buildings near the centre of the island they'll likely be on this road."

"Here is a spring!" exclaimed Sam, a minute later. "Say, that water looks good. I am going to have a drink."

All stopped to quench their thirst, for the day had been warm in spite of the breeze that was blowing.

"Look!" cried Dick, as he pointed at the wet ground. "Somebody has been here before us."

"That's so!" returned Tom. "Now, if we were only Indians, we would know whose footprints those were and would follow 'em."

Dick and Sam got down to examine the footprints. The majority of them were of good size, but a few were small, the heel marks especially so.

"I believe those marks were made by a woman's shoes!" murmured Dick. "And if so——"

"They were made by Mrs. Stanhope!" finished Sam. "Dick, I think we've struck the right trail!"

"This proves that what that young fellow of the motor boat said was not true," said Dick. "Other folks are on this island."

"Let us follow up the footmarks!" cried Larry Dixon. "Come on, messmates, to the rescue!" And he waved a stick he had picked up.

To follow up the footmarks was not easy, for they led from the dirt to the path and then to some smooth rocks. But they managed to get the general direction, which was something.

"I wonder if it would do any good to set up a yell," said Tom. "Maybe Mrs. Stanhope would hear it, and answer it."

"If she got the chance." said Sam. "If she didn't, all the yelling would do would be to let our enemies know we were here."

"No, we had better go ahead as quietly as we can," said Dick. "If possible, we want to take them unawares."

Much to their surprise, at the other side of the smooth rocks was another path, running between a thick growth of pines. Here the going was somewhat uncertain, and they had to proceed slowly, for fear of stepping into a crevice and twisting an ankle.

"If they brought Mrs. Stanhope this way, it must have been very hard on her," murmured Tom.

"Listen!" exclaimed Sam, suddenly, and held up his hand.

All became silent, and listened with strained ears. But the only sounds that reached them was the breeze through the trees, and the washing of the waves on the rocks.

"What was it, Sam?" asked Dick, in a whisper.

"I thought I heard a call."

"You must have been mistaken."

"Maybe I was, but—There it goes again!"

"That's so!" exclaimed Tom. "Somebody is calling from the other side of this patch of trees."

"It is Jerry Koswell," said Dick.

"Who is he calling to?" asked Sam.

"I don't know. Keep still and maybe we'll find out."

And then all listened with bated breath for what might follow.

CHAPTER XXVI

A TALK OF IMPORTANCE

"I say, you on the rocks! Come down here and let us talk to you!" shouted Jerry Koswell.

"Who are you. What do you want?" asked a voice that was strange to the Rovers.

"We want to know what you are doing on this island?" demanded another person, Alfred Darkingham.

"What business is it of yours?"

"What business?" shouted Darkingham, wrathfully. "A good deal of my business. This island belongs to my uncle and you have no right here."

"Oh, is that so!" exclaimed the stranger. "I didn't know that this island belonged to anybody in particular."

"Well, it does. Who are you anyway?"

"Oh, my name is of no account, since we are not acquainted," answered the stranger. "If this is your island, I suppose the only thing for me to do is to get off of it."

"What are you doing here?"

"Why—er—only looking around," stammered the stranger.

"Are you alone?"

"Can't you see that I am?"

"How did you get here?" asked Larkspur, who had come up. "We didn't see you land."

"Oh, I came in a—er—in a motor boat, run by a friend of mine. He—er—he said he would call for me later," stammered the stranger.

The Rover boys listened to this conversation with interest, and gradually drew closer, as the stranger came from the rocks to talk to Darkingham and the others.

"Say, are you the fellow who abducted a lady!" cried Larkspur.

At this direct question the stranger started. "Why—er—what makes you ask—er—that question?" he stammered.

"We know some fellows who are looking for a lady who was abducted—at least, that is the story they told," answered Koswell.

"Where did you see those fellows?" asked the stranger, and now he was plainly excited.

"They were here awhile ago."

"Here—on this island?"

"At the dock—but they didn't land—we didn't let 'em," said Larkspur.

"Humph!" The stranger was thoughtful for a moment. "No, I don't know anything about a lady who was abducted," he said slowly. "I am just roaming around a bit. As soon as my friend comes back with the motor boat I'll leave the island. If I had known it was private property I shouldn't have come ashore at all."

"Oh, I don't mind a fellow roaming around a little," said Alfred Darkingham, loftily. "But we came here to camp out, and of course we prefer to have the island to ourselves."

"I see. Well—er—I shan't disturb you. I—er—left my fishing outfit on the opposite shore. I'll go and get it, and then I'll be ready to leave as soon as my friend comes for me."

"Oh, you needn't be in such a tremendous hurry, Mr.——"

"Smith—plain John Smith," filled in the stranger. "I'm stopping at Peak's Island."

"My name is Alfred Darkingham. These are my friends, Jerry Koswell and Bart Larkspur."

"Koswell!" cried the stranger, in considerable surprise. "Did you say Jerry Koswell."

"Yes."

"Did you—were you a student at Brill College?" asked the man who had given his name as John Smith.

"Why, yes," was the reply. "But I don't remember you."

"No, for you never met me. But I have heard of you, and I think I have heard of your friend, Mr. Larkspur. Didn't you once have some trouble with some fellow students named Rover?"

"Yes," answered Larkspur, and his brow darkened.

"Pretty bad trouble, too, wasn't it?"

"Bad enough," growled Koswell. "Are you a friend to the Rovers?" he added, suspiciously.

"Oh, no, I don't know them. But I heard of the trouble."

"It was the Rovers' fault," said Jerry Koswell, sourly. "They put it off on us, but they were to blame. We might have gone back to Brill, but we didn't think it was worth while; did we, Bart?"

"No, we had enough of the grind as it was," answered Larkspur, glibly.

"Great Scott! just listen to that!" whispered Tom to his brothers. They were behind some nearby bushes and could catch every word that was spoken.

"Hush! or they may hear you," was the warning, from Dick.

"Didn't you once get a letter or two from a party named Tad Sobber?" went on the fellow who called himself John Smith.

"I did!" cried Jerry Koswell. "Then you know Sobber?"

"Supposing I told you that I did?" And the strange man eyed Koswell narrowly.

"Sobber wanted me to help him get square on the Rovers," went on Jerry Koswell.

"But you didn't want to help him, is that it?"

"Yes, I did want to help him. I sent him a long letter to that effect, but he never answered it."

"A letter that you would help Sobber?"

"Sure. The Rovers treated me dirt mean, and I'd go out of my way a good deal to get square."

"So would I!" cried Larkspur.

"I don't believe Sobber ever got your letter," went on the stranger. "He told me he had waited to hear from you but you hadn't answered."

"Then the letter got lost," answered Jerry Koswell. "I am sorry if it did, for I wanted to fix the Rovers."

"And so did I," echoed Larkspur.

"Well, maybe you can fix them yet," went on the fellow who had called himself John Smith. "You say you are going to camp out here?"

"Yes."

"Then I may see you again in the near future. I am going to Peak's Island and then to Portland, and I may see Tad Sobber, and if I do, I'll tell him what you've said."

"Do it!" cried Koswell promptly. "And tell him I am willing to help him all I can against the Rovers."

"And tell him that Bart Larkspur will help him, too," supplemented that individual.

"All right," answered the stranger. "Of course you know it might be a—er—a little risky, getting the best of those Rovers."

"Oh, we'll take a little risk," answered Koswell. "But, say!" he almost shouted. "I begin to smell a mouse!"

"Eh?"

"It was the Rovers who were here—looking for that lady who was abducted!"

"Well?"

"Did you and Sobber bring her here? Is she here now?" went on Koswell, quickly.

"If—er—if Sobber was here, would you like to meet him?"

"Sure I would. And the lady who was abducted——"

"I can't tell you anything about her. But—well, I might as well admit it—Tad Sobber is on this island with me. He—er—he came on rather a peculiar errand and he didn't want anybody to know it. But I rather think, as you are going to camp out here, he would like to meet you and talk to you."

"Where is he?"

"Up the shore a distance. If you'll wait for me here I'll hunt him up and bring him to you."

"Bring him down to our camp yonder," put in Alfred Darkingham. "We are going down there to get something to eat."

"All right, I'll bring him to your camp just as soon as I can locate him. We'll be there in less than an hour. So long!" And with a wave of his hand, the stranger turned and hurried across the rocks and into the bushes.

"I think I know that man!" whispered Sam, excitedly. "His name is Pally, Jim Pally. He was one of the freight thieves who was in league with Sid Merrick and Tad Sobber. He got away when the gang was rounded up," he added, referring to a happening, the particulars of which were related in "The Rover Boys on the Farm."

"And now he is aiding Sobber again," said Tom. "Maybe he is the fellow who helped in carrying Mrs. Stanhope off."

"I think he is the rascal who got the fortune at the lumber company office," whispered Dick. "His appearance tallies with the description Mrs. Stanhope left. Come on, let us follow him. I think he will lead us directly to where Sobber and Crabtree are, and Mrs. Sobber and Mrs. Stanhope, too."

And Dick led the way with the others at his heels.

CHAPTER XXVII

WHAT HAPPENED IN THE CAVE

The man ahead hurried along over the rocks so quickly that the Rovers and Larry Dixon had difficulty in keeping up with him.

"He's a bird for moving," was the old sailor's comment. "Splice my main brace! but I wish he'd put a reef or two in his legs!"

The man ahead suddenly made a turn around some rocks. The boys and the tar followed cautiously, so as not to be surprised.

"Wait here, I'll look ahead and investigate," said Dick. And he shoved some bushes aside.

A surprise awaited him—but not of the sort he had anticipated. The man had disappeared!

Vainly did Dick look in all directions for him. He was as completely gone as if the earth had opened and swallowed him up.

"Can he have entered some opening in the rocks?" the youth asked himself.

With added caution he moved forward a few steps further. Then, between some dense bushes, he saw a slit in some high rocks. The slit was irregular in shape but not over a foot wide in any one place.

"What do you see?" asked Tom, who, growing impatient, had followed his big brother.

"He seems to have disappeared, Tom," was the low reply.

"Did he go in there?"

"That is just what I was wondering."

Dick looked into the slit. It was of uncertain depth and looked dark and uninviting. Then the whole crowd searched the neighborhood. Not a trace of the stranger was discernable anywhere.

"Well, he didn't fly up in the air," said Sam. "He must have gone somewhere. Why not look into that opening, Dick?"

"You look out that you don't get shot!" warned Tom. "That fellow, if he is one of the old freight thieves and the rascal who robbed Mrs. Stanhope of the valise with the fortune, must be a desperate character."

"If I go in, it will be pistol first," answered Dick, grimly.

He drew the weapon Captain Wells had loaned him, and slowly but cautiously wormed his way between the rocks. It was so dark he had to feel his way along, and, fearing that he might fall into some hole, he did not advance a step until he was sure of his footing.

"Shall we come?" called Tom, softly.

"Not yet," answered Dick.

He passed along a distance of fifteen or twenty feet. Then the passageway widened, and he found himself standing on a rocky flooring that was comparatively smooth.

"Gracious! can this be one of the entrances to the smugglers' cave they told about?" he mused.

He continued to advance, and presently caught sight of a flicker of light, playing over the uneven rocks that formed the roof of the cavern.

"That must come from a campfire!" he murmured. "And if it does. I must have struck the right spot. Maybe this is where they are holding Dora's mother a prisoner!"

He continued to go forward, and the light of the fire grew brighter. Then of a sudden, he heard a step behind him.

"Will spy on me, will you!" cried a voice, vindictively, and in a trice he was struck a blow on the back of the head. He went down in a heap, and a man leaped on top of him and held him fast. Then commenced a fierce struggle, in the midst of which Dick's pistol went off, making a tremendous report in that confined space. The bullet struck the rocks, doing no damage.

The pistol had been close to Dick's head and the discharge caused the smoke to get into his face, choking and blinding him. Then he received another blow, and for a minute or two knew no more.

"Listen!" cried Tom, as the pistol went off. "Dick must be in trouble! Come on, Sam!"

"Yes, but be careful," was the answer.

"Want me?" asked the old tar, anxiously.

"You had better stay on guard here, for the present," replied Tom.

"Just as you say, messmate."

Tom wormed his way between the rocks and Sam followed. The pistol shot was followed by silence, and the two Rover boys did not know what to make of it.

"Shall I call?" asked Sam.

"Might as well," was Tom's reply, and both called Dick's name as loudly as they could.

"Help! help!" came back faintly.

"We are coming!" yelled Tom, rushing forward. "Where are you?"

"I am her——" was the answer, and then of a sudden all became quiet again, as a hand was placed over Dick's mouth.

With their weapons ready for use, Tom and Sam ran through the cavern. But all was silent, and the flickering rays from the campfire beyond were too faint for them to see much.

"Dick! Dick! Where are you?" called out Tom.

"To the left!" was the faint reply. "Turn to the left!"

The voice sounded muffled, as if the speaker was being strangled, and with their hearts in their throats, Tom and Sam advanced and at a break in the rocky wall, turned to the left. Hardly had they gone a dozen steps when they plunged downward into space.

"Oh!" came from both, and then followed a mighty splash, as the pair struck the water. Each went down over his head, and on coming up had to strike out to keep from drowning.

"Sam! Sam!" cried Tom.

"I'm here!" was the spluttered-out reply. "Are you hurt?"

"Not much, but I went over my head in water!"

"So did I."

"Where is Dick?"

"I don't know."

"Can he be drowned?"

"Oh, don't say that!"

It was pitch dark, and only by calling to each other did the two lads manage to get together. Both swam around until their feet touched a rock and on this they stood to catch their breath. The water was all around them.

"Which way did we come, Tom?" asked Sam, after a moment of silence, during which both did what they could to get back their breath.

"I don't know. I can't see a thing, can you?"

"No."

"I don't believe Dick is here."

"Neither do I, Tom. I believe somebody fooled us."

"That's it! And we fell right into the trap!"

"But where can Dick be?"

"Most likely a prisoner of our enemies," muttered Tom, bitterly.

Tom's surmise was correct, Dick was indeed a prisoner of their enemies. He had his hands and his feet bound tightly, and he had been dragged, by Tad Sobber towards the campfire that was burning at the further end of the big cave. In the meantime the fellow who had been followed by Dick went off to make sure that Tom and Sam would turn to the left and fall into the water.

"Well, Dick Rover, this is what you get for following us!" cried Tad Sobber, in tones of triumph. "Perhaps, some day, you'll learn enough to keep your hands out of my affairs."

"Sobber, tell me, what have you done with Mrs. Stanhope?" asked Dick, quickly. Even though he felt bruised and shook up, the welfare of Dora's mother was uppermost in his mind.

"I am not here to answer your questions."

"You won't tell me?"

"Not a word."

"Do you realize that you and Josiah Crabtree have committed a big crime?"

"We have done nothing wrong."

"Don't you call stealing and abducting wrong?"

"I haven't stolen anything. The fortune from Treasure Isle belonged to my uncle and me—the Stanhopes had no right to it whatsoever."

"I think otherwise—and so did the courts."

"Bah! Your side didn't treat me fairly, you bought up the judges! I know you!" stormed Tab Sobber. "The fortune was ours! Now I've got it—and I mean to keep it!"

"And what of Mrs. Stanhope?"

"Mrs. Stanhope has acted like a sensible woman."

"Acted like a sensible woman? What do you mean?"

"She has done what she should have done years ago—she has given her heart to the man who loves her."

"Sobber, you don't mean——" Dick could not go on, for the lump that came into his throat.

"I do mean it."

"What?"

"I mean that she has become the wife of Mr. Josiah Crabtree!" cried Tad Sobber. "So if you ever marry Dora Stanhope you'll have Mr. Crabtree for your father-in-law."

CHAPTER XXVIII

AT THE BOTTOM OF THE POOL

At the announcement of Tad Sobber, Dick could only stare at the speaker for the time being.

Was it really true that Dora's mother had married the disreputable Josiah Crabtree after all? It made his heart sick to think of such a state of affairs.

"You are telling me the truth?" he asked at last.

"Certainly."

"I don't believe you, Tad Sobber."

"Very well—you can ask Mr. Crabtree—and Mrs. Stanhope, when you see her."

"If she married Crabtree she was forced to do it."

"No, she married him willingly."

"I'll never believe it. Where is she now?"

"I am not here to answer questions, Dick Rover. You and your brothers came here I suppose to get the best of us. Well, you are nicely caught."

"What are you going to do with me?"

"You'll find that out before you are many hours older," answered Sobber, and turned away.

A quarter of an hour went by and the man who had met Koswell and the others outside of the cavern came back.

"Well, Jim, what about the other Rovers?" questioned Tad Sobber.

"Safe enough," answered Jim Pally, with a grin.

"Where?"

"Down in the pool."

"They slipped in?"

"They sure did."

"I hope they won't drown," went on Sobber, uneasily.

"Oh, they are safe enough. I heard 'em swimming around until they found the rocks to stand on."

"Good enough. Now, what do you think we had better do with this one?"

"Why don't you make him join his brothers?" answered Jim Pally. And then he motioned Sobber to one side, out of Dick's hearing. A conversation in a low tone followed. Pally was telling Sobber they had better be on guard, since the Rovers might not be alone. Then he told of the meeting with Koswell, Larkspur and Darkingham; and the two went off to consult with Josiah Crabtree.

Left to himself, Dick tried his best to free himself of the bonds that held him. But the work of making him a prisoner had been done well, and all he did was to cut his wrists and his ankles.

When Sobber and Pally came back they were accompanied by Josiah Crabtree. The former teacher and jailbird wore the same dictatorial look as of yore.

"Ha! so we meet again, Rover!" cried Josiah Crabtree, pursing up his lips.

"Mr. Crabtree, is it true that you have married Mrs. Stanhope?" asked Dick, bluntly.

"Well—er—we are as good as married, yes," he stammered, taken somewhat off his guard by the suddenness of the question.

"As good as married? What do you mean?"

"I mean she has promised to be my—er—my bride as soon as we can obtain a—er—a minister to perform the ceremony."

"You are forcing her into this marriage!"

"Not at all, young man, not at all! She is going to marry me of her own free will."

"I do not believe it."

"Ha! don't dare to talk to me in this fashion, Rover!" stormed Josiah Crabtree, glaring at the helpless youth before him.

"Will you let me speak to Mrs. Stanhope?"

"And poison her mind against me? Indeed not!"

"Where is she?"

"She is in safe hands."

"In your hands?"

"No, in the hands of a very estimable lady, who is doing all that is possible to make her comfortable."

"Is she well?"

"She is—er—a little bit fatigued by her journey, that is all. She will be quite herself after she has rested for a few days."

"Mr. Crabtree, you had no right to abduct her."

"Who says I abducted her? She accompanied me willingly, Rover."

"I do not believe that, and never will believe it. You mesmerized or hypnotized her, or something of the sort. I know your tricks of old."

"Ha! don't dare to talk to me in that fashion!" stormed Josiah Crabtree. "Don't you dare to do it!" And coming closer he shook his fist in Dick's face.

"You'd not do that if I were free, Josiah Crabtree!" cried the youth, defiantly.

"Say, we can't afford to waste time in talk!" interrupted Tad Sobber. "I reckon the best thing we can do with this fellow is to make him join his brothers."

"And then—" went on Crabtree, and finished in a whisper which Dick did not catch.

A few minutes later Dick was led back into the cavern towards the pool into which his brothers had fallen. Sobber carried a torch, that threw a flickering light throughout the dismal underground opening.

"Help! help!" came faintly from the bottom of the pool, and looking down those on the rocks high above saw Sam and Tom standing there, in water up to their knees.

"Hello!" cried Dick. "Are you all right?"

"We would be, if we could get out," answered Tom.

"Hello! It's the Sobber crowd, with Dick!" murmured Sam.

"I don't think they are going to aid us," returned Tom.

A few words passed between Sobber, Crabtree, and Pally, and then while two of the evildoers held Dick the third cut his bonds.

"Now, then, you can join your brothers!" cried Sobber, and gave Dick a shove that sent him headlong. Down he came with a tremendous splash, and then the waters of the pool closed over him.

"You cowards!" shouted Tom, in a rage. "I shouldn't treat a dog that way!"

"You shut your mouth!" yelled back Tad Sobber. "It serves you right—for following us."

"Some day you'll be in jail, Tad Sobber!" shouted Sam. "It's where you belong."

All waited for Dick to come up, but second after second passed and the eldest Rover boy failed to appear.

"Something is wrong!" gasped Tom, in alarm. "Maybe his head struck on the bottom," cried Sam. "If he is dead, you'll pay the penalty!" he cried, to those on the shore of the rocky pool.

All were worried, for those above had not expected anything of this sort to happen. They looked down, but could see nothing of Dick.

"I'm going to hunt for him!" cried Tom, and leaving the rocks upon which he was standing, he swam with all haste in the direction of the spot where his big brother had gone down. Seeing this, Sam followed his example.

"Perhaps we had better be getting out of here!" muttered Jim Pally, turning pale.

"No! no! let us see if they bring Dick Rover up!" answered Tad Sobber, hoarsely.

The firebrand was swung into a larger blaze and the glare cast on the waters. As the rays lit up the weird scene, Tom set up a sudden shout.

"There he is!"

"Where?" demanded Sam.

"Over yonder! I just saw him bob up. Quick, Sam, before he goes to the bottom!"

The brothers swam to the spot indicated by Tom with all possible speed, and Tom made a dive under the surface. When he came up again he had hold of Dick's left foot.

"I've go—got him!" he gasped. "Hel—help me!"

For reply Sam ranged up by his brother's side, and between them they raised Dick up and swam with him to the spot where the water was shallow. Then they stood there, in water up to their knees, supporting Dick as best they could. The oldest Rover boy was all but unconscious.

"Going to help us?" yelled Tom, to their enemies.

"What's the matter with him?" asked Tad Sobber.

"Oh, I fancy he was only shamming!" came from Josiah Crabtree. "Come on away."

"Don't you dare to leave us here!" cried Sam.

"Help us out," came from Tom. "It is your duty to do it."

"Not much!" answered Tad Sobber, with a sneer. "You can help yourself—if you can!" And with these words he walked away, in company with Crabtree and Pally, leaving the Rovers to their fate in the water and the darkness.

CHAPTER XXIX

A MINUTE TOO LATE

"Of all the rascals!" murmured Tom, as the light faded from sight.

"They are the worst!" supplemented Sam. And then he added: "How do you feel Dick?"

"Oh, I—I guess I'll come around!" murmured the oldest Rover boy. "But I came pretty close to being drowned!" he added, with a shudder. "I struck something and it about stunned me, and I swallowed a lot of water."

Tom and Sam continued to hold up their brother until Dick had recovered sufficiently to support himself. As they stood on the submerged rocks, they listened for some sound from their enemies, but none came.

"Maybe they have left the cave," suggested Sam, after ten or fifteen minutes had passed.

"This is a fierce place," was Tom's comment. "It's just like a great big well!"

"And we are like the frogs at the bottom of the well!" added Dick, grimly. He felt a little weak, but otherwise was all right.

"I looked around when we had the light of that torch," said Tom, "but I didn't see any place where a fellow could climb out, did you?"

"Nary a spot, Tom," answered Sam. "The walls were all as smooth and as slippery as glass."

"Do you think they mean to leave us here to die?" asked Dick.

"I shouldn't think they'd be as heartless as all that," came from Tom. "They'd be afraid of consequences."

An hour went by—just then it was an age—and at last the boys saw a glimmer of light approaching. It flickered and flared over the walls for fully a minute and then commenced to fade.

"Somebody went past, through the main cave!" cried Tom. "Wonder who it was?"

"The Sobber crowd most likely," returned Dick.

"But it might be somebody else!" cried Sam. "I'm going to yell and find out."

He raised his voice in a loud call, and Tom and Dick joined in. Several minutes went by, and they called again. Then they saw the flickering of the light once more.

"Who is there?" came faintly to their ears.

"This way! This way!" shouted one Rover boy after another.

"Be careful of where you step!" cautioned Tom.

"Where are you?"

"This way!" they answered, and kept calling until the light of a ship's lantern came into view, and they saw Captain Wells and Larry Dixon approaching.

"Well, I never!" ejaculated the captain of the steam tug, as he came to a halt on the brink of the blackish pool. "How in the world did you git down there?"

"Help us out first, and then we'll tell you," replied Dick, quickly.

"Didn't you meet our enemies?" asked Tom.

"Nary a soul have we met since we landed," answered the captain.

"Which way did you enter the cave?" asked Sam.

"By the slit in the rocks—where you came in," answered Larry Dixon. "I watched you disappear, and afterwards I heard some yelling. Then I got scared and ran down to the shore and signalled for the steam tug to come in. I told the cap'n all I knew, and he came ashore with a lantern to see what was wrong—and here we be."

"You've come in the nick of time," said Dick. "Our enemies, the Sobber crowd, are here, and they left us as you see us. I rather think they have Mrs. Stanhope and that fortune here, too, but I am not certain. Help to get us out of here, and we'll get after 'em without delay."

"Don't know how we are going to help you without a rope," said the captain.

"I saw some rope, down in the big part of this cave," said Larry Dixon. "Let me have the light an' I'll fetch it in a jiffy!"

He took the light and was off on the run. When he returned he was out of breath. In his hands he held several pieces of good, stout rope, parts of the same rope which had been used to make Dick a close prisoner.

"We can splice these," said the old tar, and while Captain Wells held the lantern, he tied the bits together. Then both he and the captain allowed one end of the rope to dangle down into the hole, while they braced themselves and held on to the upper portion.

"Is it long enough?" asked Captain Wells.

"I think so—I'll see," cried Tom, and leaving the rocks he swam over to the rope. He was just able to reach it, and being something of an athlete, went up the rope hand over hand, with his feet against the rocks for added support.

"Now you go, Dick!" cried Sam. "If you are weak and fall, I'll catch you."

It was quite a task for Dick to gain the rocks at the top of the pool and once he came close to giving up and slipping back into the water. But he was gritty, and Tom assisted him by leaning down on his breast and extending a helping hand. Then Sam came up, and the three Rovers stood beside the two men who had come to their rescue.

"Phew! I am glad we are out of that!" murmured Sam, as he looked back at the cold and gruesome waters.

"We don't want to stay here!" cried Dick. "We want to get after the Sobber crowd—before they have a chance to leave the island!"

"How can they leave the island?" questioned Sam. "I don't think they have a boat. I haven't seen any."

"But Jerry Koswell's crowd has a boat, Sam—that swift motor craft."

"Do you think they would aid such criminals as Sobber and Crabtree?"

"They might—just to get the best of us."

"Then the sooner we get after our enemies the better."

"Where are your pistols?" asked the captain of the steam tug.

"Mine was taken from me by Sobber," answered Dick.

"And ours are at the bottom of the pool," added Sam. "We both dropped 'em when we plunged into the water." And then he and his brothers acquainted Captain Wells and the old sailor with the particulars of their adventures since entering the cavern.

"Well, I still have my pistol!" cried Captain Wells, grimly.

"And I've got a good club," came from Larry Dixon.

"We can arm ourselves with clubs," said Dick. "But the main thing just now is to keep those rascals in sight. If they slip us, there will be no telling where they will go to."

With eyes and ears on the alert, the whole party made its way through the big cave, coming out of the main opening, not far from where the campfire still lay smouldering.

"They certainly left in a hurry," remarked Tom, as he gazed around. "They didn't wait to pick up all of their provisions."

"I guess they got scared," murmured Dick. "Well, they'll get more scared when they find we are so close on their heels."

"Where do you suppose they went to?" asked the captain.

"I don't know. But I think the best thing to do is to go down to where that motor boat was tied up. I don't think they can leave unless they use that boat—unless, of course, they have some craft we haven't as yet seen."

There was a well-defined path running from the cave down to the shore of the island. This they followed, through the patch of woods and over some rocks. Then they came to an opening where were located several dilapidated buildings. Not far from one building were the remains of a recent camp.

"I believe this was the camp Darkingham and those with him made!" ejaculated Dick. "They have gone—maybe they have left the island!"

"Come on, I don't like this!" put in Tom, and broke into a run for the old dock, and the others followed on his heels.

They were still a hundred yards from the dock when Tom let up a shout:

"There they are!"

"Where?" asked Dick.

"In the motor boat!"

"Who?" questioned Sam.

"The Sobber crowd—and they have Mrs. Stanhope with them."

"Stop! stop!" yelled Dick, at the top of his voice. "Stop, I tell you! Mrs. Stanhope!"

"Oh!" came from the lady, as she espied the Rovers. "Save me! Save me! Don't let them take me further away!"

"Put on all speed!" roared Tad Sobber, to Pally, who was at the engine. "Crowd her to the limit! They are after us!"

"Here we go! Hold fast everybody!" answered Pally, and the next moment the motor boat shot out into the waters of Casco Bay.

CHAPTER XXX

BACK HOME—CONCLUSION

"Too late!" groaned Dick. "Oh, why didn't we get here a minute sooner!"

"Stop, you rascals!" sang out Captain Wells. "Stop, or I'll fire!" and he raised his pistol.

"Don't shoot! You might hit Mrs. Stanhope!" whispered Dick.

"I only want to scare 'em," muttered the captain of the steam tug.

The motor boat gathered headway rapidly, and soon was out of range of the pistol. The Rovers saw that the craft contained Tad Sobber, Jim Pally, Josiah Crabtree and Mrs. Stanhope and another woman, probably Mrs. Sobber.

"Wonder what has become of Koswell, Larkspur and that Darkingham," said Sam.

"I don't know, and I don't care, just now!" returned Dick. "Captain, we must follow that boat without delay. If they get out of our sight we may never get another chance to rescue Mrs. Stanhope!"

"I'll get after 'em as soon as I can," returned the master of the steam tug.

But to start a pursuit was not so easy, from the fact that the tug lay on the other side of the island and could not be signalled.

"Tom and I can go after the tug," said Sam. "The rest of you can try to keep that motor boat in sight;" and so it was arranged.

The two Rover boys skirted the south end of Chesoque Island. They kept on a run, and on turning a corner of rocks, plumped fairly and squarely into Koswell, Larkspur and Darkingham, who were talking earnestly among themselves.

"They said they would send the boat back sure," Koswell was saying, when Tom almost ran him down.

"Hello! you here!" cried Tom, and then, as Koswell grabbed him by the arm he added: "Let me go!"

"Not so fast!" roared Koswell. "Bart, catch the other fellow!"

"I will!" muttered Bart Larkspur, and caught Sam by the arm.

What followed, came with such swiftness that both Koswell and Larkspur were taken completely off their guard. Tom drew back and hit Koswell a blow in the nose that sent him staggering back against the rocks and made the blood spurt freely. Sam, seeing this, also struck out, reaching Larkspur's left eye, and putting that optic in deep mourning. Larkspur fell back on Darkingham, and for the moment there was great confusion.

"Skip! We don't want to be delayed!" cried Tom, to his brother, and on they went again, before their enemies had time to recover.

Inside of five minutes they came in sight of the steam tug. Those aboard were on the watch for the return of Captain Wells, and the engineer had a full head of steam up, to use in case of emergency.

"Quick!" cried Tom, as he and Sam rushed on board. "Captain Wells and my brother want you on the other side of the island at once!"

"We'll get there as quick as the propeller can take us," said the mate, and the engineer nodded to show that he understood. The tug backed away from the island, and in a moment more was on the way to the old dock.

"Say we gave Koswell and Larkspur something to remember us by," remarked Sam, grimly.

"So we did," answered Tom, with a grin. "Wish it had been ten times as much!"

"They and that Darkingham must have loaned the motor boat to the Sobber crowd."

"Most likely Sobber paid 'em well for its use. He could do it easily—out of that fortune."

As the steam tug rounded the end of the island, Tom and Sam were just able to see the motor boat in the distance. It seemed to be heading for the mainland.

"All aboard!" sang out Tom, as they ran up to the old dock. But this

BACK HOME—CONCLUSION

invitation was unnecessary, for Dick, Captain Wells and Larry Dixon leaped on the deck as soon as the craft was close enough.

"Now then, after her!" sang out the eldest Rover boy. "Crowd on all steam! I'll pay all expenses, and more!"

"Even if she blows up?" queried the captain, with a bit of dry humor.

"Yes, even if she blows up, Captain! Oh, we must catch them!" added Dick, pleadingly.

"We'll do our level best, Mr. Rover. Nobody could do more."

Soon the throbbing of the engine showed that the tug was running under a full pressure of steam. The spray dashed all over the craft and those on board, but to this nobody paid attention. Every eye was riveted on the craft ahead.

Those on the motor boat were equally eager, and watched the pursuit with chagrin.

"Do you—er—think they will catch us?" asked Josiah Crabtree, nervously, not once but several times.

"I don't know—I hope not," answered Pally.

"Can't we run faster?"

"I am crowding her to the limit now."

"Do you know about motor boats? Perhaps Mr. Sobber knows more."

"I don't," answered Tad Sobber. "Wish I did."

"I know about 'em—I ran one for two summers," answered Jim Pally. "I'll leave 'em behind if it's in the boat to do it."

"Oh, please let me go!" cried Mrs. Stanhope, almost tearfully. "Mr. Crabtree, I do not want to go with you another step! Please let me go!"

"Keep quiet, Mrs. Stanhope, don't excite yourself," he answered, trying to soothe her. But he was so nervous his voice trembled as he spoke. He had not dreamed that the pursuit would become so swift and sure.

Closer and closer drew the steam tug, until those on board could plainly see all that was taking place on the motor boat.

"I command you to stop!" yelled Captain Wells. "Stop, or we'll run you down."

"No, no, don't you do that!" screamed Josiah Crabtree, in fright.

"Save me! Oh, save me!" screamed Mrs. Stanhope, and then, of a sudden, she sprang to her feet, leaped to the stern deck of the motor boat, and cast herself headlong into the waters of the bay.

The movement was so unexpected by the others on the Magnet that not a hand was raised to detain her. She went down, directly in the path of the oncoming tug.

"Stop! Back her!" screamed Dick, in horror, and Tom and Sam also yelled out a warning. There was a quick jangling of a bell, and the engine was stopped. Then the power was reversed, and the steam tug was steered to one side.

"There she is!" cried Tom, pointing with his hand, and the next instant came a splash, as Dick made a dive overboard. He, too, had seen Mrs. Stanhope floating near, and soon he had her in his arms and was supporting her.

The engine of the tug was now stopped, and a rope was thrown to the eldest Rover boy, and he and Mrs. Stanhope were hauled on board. As the lady was brought on deck, she fainted away, but in a few minutes she recovered.

"Thank heaven, she is safe!" murmured Dick.

"I'm thankful we didn't run her down!" added Captain Wells. "It was a close shave! We had to reverse like lightning."

"It was well done, sir," answered Sam.

"Couldn't have been better," came from Tom.

"But, say, aren't we going after those rascals? Remember, even though we have rescued Mrs. Stanhope, they still have the fortune!"

"Sure, we are going after 'em!" cried Dick. "Go ahead!"

The order to proceed was given, but, much to the captain's chagrin, the tug refused to get up any speed. Then came a report from the engineer that the sudden reversing of the engine had broken some of the machinery. They could run, but it would have to be slowly.

"Then they'll get away after all!" groaned Sam. "And with that fortune, too!"

"Fortune?" came from Mrs. Stanhope, who was standing near the

"THERE SHE IS!" CRIED TOM! AND THE NEXT INSTANT CAME A SPLASH, AS DICK MADE A DIVE OVERBOARD.

boiler, trying to dry her wet garments. "What about the fortune, boys?"

"Haven't they got that fortune with them?" questioned Tom, quickly.

"Oh, no, they buried it, in the cave on the island," was the answer. "They didn't know I saw them, but I did. Tad Sobber and Mr. Crabtree said they would come back, after—after—" And here she blushed deeply.

"After old Crabtree had forced you to marry him, I suppose," whispered Dick.

"Yes, Dick. But, oh! I didn't want to do it! He tried to hypnotize me, just as he tried to do years ago—but I fought him off as best I could!" answered Mrs. Stanhope, earnestly.

"He ought to be in prison again!" muttered Dick.

"If the fortune is on the island, let us go and get it," cried Sam. "We can't catch that motor boat anyway!" For the craft was now all but out of sight.

The steam tug was headed for Chesoque Island, and slowly made her way to the old dock. There the engineer and his assistant set to work to make the necessary repairs, while the three Rover boys and Mrs. Stanhope visited the cave. Once in the underground opening, the lady pointed out the spot where the valise containing the fortune had been secreted between the rocks.

"Here it is!" cried Tom, and dragged the valise to light.

"Open it and see if the fortune is safe!" came from Sam, in a voice he tried in vain to steady.

The key to the valise was missing, so the lock to the bag had to be broken open. Inside were the gold and precious stones.

"All here—or at least the greater portion of it," was Dick's comment, and he was right. Only about five hundred dollars in gold was missing, and two small diamonds—hardly worth mentioning beside the total value of the treasure.

"Hurrah!" shouted Tom. "We've beaten them after all! We've got the treasure!"

"And Mrs. Stanhope," added Dick. "We must send word to Dora and the others just as soon as we can!"

"It's a pity we didn't catch those rascals," murmured Sam.

"Oh, we'll get them some time!" said Dick. How they fell in with their enemies again will be related in another volume of this series, to be entitled, "The Rover Boys in the Air; or, From College Campus to the Clouds," a tale telling the particulars of several happenings far out of the ordinary.

While the steam tug was laid up for repairs, several of the party took a walk and looked for Koswell, Larkspur and Darkingham. But they looked in vain, for those rascals were thoroughly frightened, and kept themselves well hidden in the woods.

That evening found the Rover boys and Mrs. Stanhope in Portland, where they put up at one of the leading hotels. Messages were sent to Dora, the Lanings, and the Rovers at home, telling of the rescue of Mrs. Stanhope, and of the recovery of the fortune. Then Mrs. Stanhope told how she had been lured from her home and abducted, and then placed in the care of Mrs. Sobber, and how she had managed to mail the postal card.

"They treated me kindly enough," she said. "But they would not let me have my liberty, and I think they told outsiders that I was insane."

"That is just what they did," answered Dick.

A general alarm was sent out for Sobber, Crabtree and the others. But they kept in the dark and were not captured.

"Oh, how glad I shall be to get back home!" murmured Mrs. Stanhope, when the return was begun. "It seems an age since I went away!"

"Dora will be glad to see you," answered Dick.

"I owe you and your brothers a great deal, Dick!" she went on earnestly. "You are all noble young men!" And this earnest praise made all of the Rover boys blush.

The return to Cedarville was a great event. Dora clasped her mother in her arms and laughed and wept by turns, and then threw herself into Dick's embrace.

"Oh, Dick! It was splendid!" she cried. "Oh, I shall never forget it, never!" And then she kissed him right in front of everybody.

The Lanings were equally pleased, and Nellie and Grace were proud of the parts Tom and Sam had played in the affair.

"You are a regular hero!" said Nellie to Tom, and gave him a glance that thrilled him through and through.

"And we shall always remember what you did!" added Grace, to Sam.

"You did better than the authorities," was Mr. Anderson Rover's comment.

"The authorities did nothing," added Mr. Laning. "If it hadn't been for your boys——" And then he bobbed his head enthusiastically. "Great lads! fine lads!" he added.

"Whoop!" cried Tom, in sudden high spirits, and catching Sam by the arms and whirling him around. "Say, I suppose now we can go back and finish that vacation, eh?"

"Sure thing, Tom!" cried Sam.

And then both set up a merry whistle; and here let us take our leave and say good-bye.

THE END

Printed in Great Britain
by Amazon